# PRAISE FOR SALLY GARDNER

'This heartbreaking, brilliantly written novel
is the most original publication for years'
*The Times*

'Shades of Sarah Waters...irresistible'
*Guardian*

'Arresting and original and written in a singular voice'
*Telegraph*

'The prize-winning Gardner is a dab
hand at literary world-creation'
*Observer*

'This is an inspirational piece of writing'
*New Statesman*

'A truly original voice...a thrilling read'
*Spectator*

'Beautiful, twisted and dark. A masterpiece'
*Big Issue*

**Sally Gardner** is an award-winning children's novelist who has sold more than two and a half million books worldwide and been translated into 22 languages. This is her third adult novel.

For more information visit www.sallygardner.co.uk
@TheSallyGardner

**Also by Sally Gardner, writing as Wray Delaney**

*AN ALMOND FOR A PARROT*
*THE BEAUTY OF THE WOLF*

# THE
# SNOW
# SONG

## Sally Gardner

ONE PLACE. MANY STORIES

HQ
An imprint of HarperCollins*Publishers* Ltd
1 London Bridge Street
London SE1 9GF

This edition 2020

1

First published in Great Britain by
HQ, an imprint of HarperCollins*Publishers* Ltd 2020

Hardback ISBN: 978-0-00-821740-2
Trade Paperback ISBN: 978-0-00-821742-6

MIX
Paper from
responsible sources
FSC
www.fsc.org
FSC™ C007454

This book is produced from independently certified FSC™ paper
to ensure responsible forest management.

For more information visit: www.harpercollins.co.uk/green

This book is set in Sabon

Printed and bound in Great Britain by
CPI Group (UK) Ltd, Croydon, CR0 4YY

To my great friend and mentor, Jane Fior, who has given me so much love and support. When I told her I didn't think I could write a book about snow, she wisely said, 'You can.'
So here it is.

I have used the term 'gypsy' in this story as it's appropriate for the time the story is set in. I mean no disrespect to the Roma who where called Tzigane in Transylvania. But whatever name is used, the Roma people have suffered prejudice and discrimination throughout the history of the world.

This is the Hour of Lead –
Remembered, if outlived,
As Freezing persons, recollect the Snow –
First – Chill – then Stupor – then the letting go –

EMILY DICKINSON

# CHAPTER ONE

## SNOW SONG

It was the sound of his violin that first cast a spell on Edith. Even before she saw him, the restless notes of his melody drew her to him. The musician was sitting on a bench outside the cobbler's, a pair of new boots beside him. The morning sunshine illuminated his outline, striking against the burnt orange of the cobbler's house. The violin looked to Edith as if it were made of liquid honey so polished was its surface. The rhythm of the song with its languid melancholy echoed her own feelings. His music danced into her heart to free her troubled soul from its cage, and she stood mesmerised.

When he had finished he looked up at her, his eyes the colour of a blue winter sky, his hair dark like her own, his face elegant in its composition. Generous lips, a straight nose – unlike the young men of her village with their blond, dumpling faces that lacked definition, as if they had all been baked in the same oven.

'What's the music called?' she asked.

'Snow Song,' he said.

'But it's spring – the snow has gone,' she felt herself blushing. Normally she would never have had the courage to speak to a stranger. It wouldn't have occurred to her to do so if it hadn't been for the violin. Or so she told herself.

He smiled at her. 'The snow will come again in time.'

This day became in Edith's mind the border between two worlds. Whatever she had been before she heard him play the Snow Song, she would no longer remember. By the time he had finished she felt she had entered her realm. She had never known what it was she wanted, now she did: she wanted to hear his music for the rest of her days. She was standing and the tune made two giddy sticks of her legs. She sat down beside him and only then did she notice his small, raggle-taggle dog. They were silent for a while.

'Do you know the secret of the violin?' he asked. 'And how it came into this world?'

'No,' said Edith, aware she was being watched by disapproving villagers hidden behind shuttered windows. None of it mattered. 'What is the secret?'

He had turned from her and was putting the violin back in its case. 'A gypsy could tell you the story of the violin's birth.'

Edith asked, 'Do you know it?'

'I do,' he said.

And she boldly asked if he might like to have supper with her and her father that evening, adding, 'You could tell us the story of the violin.'

*

The butcher, in the shadow of his doorway, was angry to see Edith talk with such ease to a stranger. Strangers weren't welcome in this village, she should know that. He made a mental note to fine the cabinet maker for it. The old drunk should keep a closer eye on his daughter. The butcher looked again and saw Edith and the stranger sitting side by side as if they had always sat that way – two beautiful creatures. He hit his fist into his hand and returned to the slaughterhouse.

*

All that day Edith felt her heart to be still dancing to the young man's music. She sacrificed one of her chickens and cooked it with great care and with great care laid the table. Only then did she tell her father of their guest. He had as usual been drinking since midday. There was plenty of work for a cabinet maker but not for a drunk who could only be trusted to finish a bottle of wine.

'I don't want a gypsy at my table,' he said.

'He isn't a gypsy,' said Edith.

'He's a stranger,' said her father. 'You know what happens when a stranger enters the house.'

Edith sighed. She'd grown up with these endless superstitions, too many to remember. 'No, what does happen?' she asked, knowingly perfectly well her father had forgotten the old tale of how the bloodless often came disguised as strangers.

He took a bottle and, holding it tight to him, said, 'On your head be it,' and went to his room.

As Edith put out the painted plates she realised she hadn't asked the musician his name or what he did to earn a living.

Her father was too drunk to stay long awake and, shortly after the young man arrived with cheese and wine, the cabinet maker excused himself.

'A gypsy if ever I saw one,' he mumbled as he went to his bed.

Edith said simply, 'He's a drunk. I've never known him not to be like that. I should've asked you your name.'

'Demetrius,' he said. 'I'm a shepherd.'

They sat down to eat and to begin with she could hardly think what to say but he said, 'I heard that this village had a great storyteller.'

'That was my grandmother. She died nearly five years ago.'

'I'm sorry to hear that. I was told she knew the story of the violin.'

'If she did, she never told me or anyone else in the village. But she had many stories she would tell. Round here, nobody wants to hear gypsy tales, more's the pity. She said she cut hers to fit the mood of the listeners.'

He laughed. 'That's what I try to do with my playing.'

It was on the tip of her tongue to say, 'You do,' but she stopped herself and asked if he would like more to eat.

'Are you a storyteller?' he said.

Edith had never thought of herself as having that gift.

True, she knew all her grandmother's stories, but the idea that she might be able to hold a crowd spellbound had never occurred to her.

'I'm too shy for that,' she said.

'But you love story and music?'

'Both,' she said. 'I know plenty of stories. It's music I thirst for.'

He sat back in the chair and for a moment she imagined them to have been long married and their children grown.

'Once,' he said, 'in a village not far from here lived a girl who all believed to be cursed because no man would ask for her hand in marriage despite her wealth and beauty. As for the girl, she was in love with a farmer who never cast a glance in her direction. She did all she could to get his attention and, seeing that her efforts were fruitless, she called on the devil. He came holding a mirror in his hand. She looked at herself in its icy glass and then the devil asked her what she wanted. She told him of her love for the farmer.

'"If that's all," said the devil, "I can help you. Bring me your father, your mother and your four brothers."

'The girl gave them up without a sigh. Out of the body of the father the devil fashioned a violin. Out of the white hairs from the mother's head he made a bow. Out of the four brothers he made the strings and strung them across the fiddle. "Now," he said, "when your beloved comes, play the instrument."

'She did, and when the farmer heard the music he fell under its spell. Never had two people been happier. Nine days passed and the young lovers were walking in the forest when the devil appeared in their path.

'"I am your lord and master," he said. "Worship me."

'"No," they said, "never."

'The devil laughed and held up his mirror. The farmer saw his reflection and knew it was too late.

'"Both of you have listened to my music," said the devil, "and both of you have looked into my mirror. Now you will have to pay the price."

'The devil carried them away and the violin lay at the crossroads in the forest until a gypsy happened to find it. He plays it still, driving men and women wild when they hear its intoxicating sound.'

'I can well believe it,' Edith said. 'Will you play again?' As Demetrius picked up his bow she thought how extraordinary it was that a piece of wood could be transformed into an instrument and the music it made could weave its way into your soul.

And slowly he played the fiddle in a key that sang to the rhythm of her very being and the yearning chords filled with longing were carried softly away into the spring night.

Only when he was leaving did he ask, 'Would you marry me?'

And she said, 'Yes.'

They stood a long while, close together, not touching. Finally he put his hand to her face and then he left.

She cleared the plates almost in a trance and knew as if she had always known that she would marry the shepherd.

# CHAPTER TWO

## A TALL TALE FROM
## THIN THREAD

Love came later, or so Edith told herself, though she wasn't sure that she believed that. Every night Demetrius sat with her on the verandah and she felt the stars had aligned to bring her the shepherd and his violin. She hadn't known until then how love could transform you. The mountain appeared more beautiful than she had ever seen it; the fresh leaves on the little walnut tree in the yard seemed greener, brighter.

Such happiness as she felt with Demetrius was intoxicating and she feared that in her passion she might lose her footing and be swept away.

'Where do I begin and where do you end?' she asked him.

He thought for a while and said, 'When two rivers collide can you tell, in that whirling water, which river was which?'

'No,' she said. 'And does it matter?'

She found in his love the healing balm she needed.

Demetrius talked to her as an equal, unlike the miller's

son who not long ago had tried to woo her with an eye on her hips and an eye on her breasts.

Demetrius told her, 'Hold up your questions. They're boulders,' and laughing said, 'Throw them down and don't be satisfied with half-thought-out answers.'

One evening he asked her to tell him a story.

'What story would you like to hear?' she said.

'You choose.'

She thought for a time and why this one came to her she couldn't say.

'There were two brothers, neither were rich nor poor. A letter arrived to tell them they had been left in their uncle's will a tall house and a chest full of gold. The letter went on to say that whichever brother arrived first, it would all be his. If the brothers arrived together, they could share it between them.

'The two brothers had never been close nor far apart and they agreed that they would set off together in the morning. But the next day the younger brother had gone. The older brother sighed and went to open his shop for business as usual. He'd had a night to sleep on things and he'd thought about the letter. Their uncle had never been a kind man and the town where they were to go had no tall houses that he could remember.

'The younger brother walked there and did not wish to arrive looking shabby so the minute he entered the town he bought himself new shoes, a suit, a coat and a hat. Not having the money, he promised to pay the cobbler, the tailor and the hatter as soon as he had the chest of gold. He decided that as he was now rich he would stay in a fine hotel, and as he had walked so far he would have a meal fit for a king. His head filled with wine, he went to claim his inheritance.

'He was pleased when he found the house for it was a grand building, though he wouldn't have described it as tall. "It doesn't matter," he said to himself. "All this will be mine and mine alone."

'A butler took him upstairs and opened a door. The room was the nursery and in the middle of the floor was a tall dolls' house and beside it a small toy chest filled with toy coins.

'"This must be a mistake," said the younger brother.

'The butler said nothing. Broken by disappointment and having no money, the younger brother tried to leave the town without paying for his new clothes, his hotel bill, or the meal fit for a king, and found himself in prison.

'The elder brother worked hard and one day he met a tall woman and fell in love. Time passed as time always will.

'The younger brother, freed from jail, took comfort in wine and bemoaned the injustice that life had thrown at him. In his sober moments he grew curious about his older brother and wondered if he, like himself, was penniless. He returned to the village and found his older brother living in the same house, happily married to the tall woman. Having no resentment, the older brother asked the younger to stay and dine with them.

'"How did you know that the will was a trick?" the younger brother asked.

'"I would have told you but you were in such a hurry to leave."

'"Told me what?" said the younger brother, his eye greedy on the wine.

'"That all the riches we have are to be discovered inside us. My wealth I found in the love I have for my wife. Such a promise as our uncle made us were hollow words from a shallow grave."'

When Edith had finished she said, 'I didn't understand that story when my grandmother first told me it. I thought it must be missing a part. I know now it is about love that lies within us. Love is greater than a tall house and chest of gold.'

Demetrius kissed her. 'You don't know how wise you are,' he said.

\*

Demetrius asked the cabinet maker for Edith's hand. The shepherd was not from these parts and therefore was considered an outsider and not a suitable husband. But in a drunken moment Edith's father weakened and gave his consent to their betrothal. With sobriety came regret.

The butcher had long let it be known that he wanted Edith for his wife. The cabinet maker, hat in hand, with a sore head and a worried heart, paid a visit to the butcher to tell him what he had done. The butcher was skinning rabbits at the time. He didn't look up from his work.

He said, 'The lambing season's nearly over.'

'That's so,' said the cabinet maker.

The butcher wiped his knife on his apron and said, 'The shepherd will soon take his flock to graze farther afield.'

The cabinet maker hadn't thought of that.

'You are her father. Tell them they can't be married until after the harvest supper and not a day before. As for Edith – make her swear on her dead mother's bible that if the shepherd isn't back by the first snowfall, she will marry me. If she does that – swear, I mean, in front of the mayor – then you can forget about the money you owe me.'

The cabinet maker walked home with a spring in his step. All would be well, he told himself. He would stop drinking, turn his business round. And with each step he began to spin himself a tall tale from thin thread.

The cabinet maker told the young couple his terms.

'Then we'll be married on St Catherine's Day,' said Demetrius.

'The saint of old maids,' said Edith.

'Can you wait that long?' the cabinet maker said to Demetrius. 'Wouldn't you like a younger girl? More available? From another village, perhaps?'

'No,' said Demetrius.

'Someone more like you?'

'In what way, like me?'

'A gypsy,' said the cabinet maker.

'I've not an ounce of gypsy blood in me,' said Demetrius, laughing. 'More's the pity.'

The cabinet maker, intending the suggestion as an insult,

hadn't expected such a response. The humour of his future son-in-law irritated him and he scurried away as might a cockroach, congratulating himself that he hadn't disclosed the last part of the butcher's request. He would tell Edith tomorrow when the shepherd was seeing to his lambs.

'I doubt you'll find that funny, gypsy,' he muttered and lifted the bottle to his lips.

The thought that he'd outwitted the shepherd pleased the cabinet maker. What could the shepherd do when he found out Edith was promised to another man? Nothing. Like the rest of us, he thought, he'll be under the butcher's boot.

That night, when they were alone, Edith gave Demetrius her gold coin. He didn't know the custom of the region and she told him it was a token of her love and represented a bond between them that couldn't be broken. He put his arms about her and held her close, and promised on his life it never would be.

'On our wedding day,' she said to him, 'we will put this coin under our mattress and there it will stay to be handed down to our daughter when it's her turn to choose a husband.'

He kissed her. 'When I come back at harvest time, I'll bring you a ring.'

'And I'll give you the red shirt that I'll sew for you to be married in.'

# CHAPTER THREE

## HER MOTHER'S BIBLE

'This is foolish,' Edith said to her father when he told her what the butcher wanted. 'I'm to be married to Demetrius. I will never marry the butcher. How much do you owe him?'

'Nothing to do with you,' said the cabinet maker. 'That's my business. But if it's not done today the butcher will forbid the elders from letting your wedding go ahead.'

'I want to speak to Demetrius first,' Edith said. 'Surely it can wait until tomorrow.'

'No, it can't,' said the cabinet maker. 'There will be no marriage unless you swear.'

Edith looked at his purple blushed face, the wine-red veins that inked his puffy features. How could this man be her father? They had nothing in common other than they lived under the same roof – and a leaky roof at that. She tried to think of one loving memory she had of him and couldn't.

'Well? What do you say?' He came towards her and she

stepped back. 'Don't you trust the gypsy to keep his word? Is that it?'

He poured himself a glass, his hands trembling. 'You'll do as you're told. Swear on your mother's bible.'

However much she hated the idea, she knew, as did every other village girl, that without the consent of the elders nothing happened in this community – and the head of the village elders was the butcher himself. Her freedom lay with the shepherd. She had to trust that Demetrius would return to her before the first snowfall.

'Why wouldn't he?' she said defiantly to herself. 'Why wouldn't he?' she said again as reluctantly she went to find her mother's bible.

'No, no,' said her father when Edith returned with it and began to take the oath. 'Not here; this has to be witnessed. It has to be proper.'

'Witnessed by whom?'

'The mayor.'

'Father, I'm marrying Demetrius.'

The cabinet maker put on his hat.

'Wait,' said Edith and before she could stop him he had taken a firm hold of her arm and they'd set off through the yard, her father kicking the hens out of his way as they went.

She noted that her father showed the same determination to have this oath done as he normally would when in search of a bottle of wine.

The mayor's house was painted yellow ochre and was far more substantial than any of the other houses. The mayor and his wife, Georgeta, had a son, a sickly young man who was away at university. The mayor employed two maids and a cook, unheard of in a small mountain village. He had been born into privilege, yet for all his fine clothes, his library and chain of office everyone knew who held the power. Not the mayor but the butcher.

One of the maids came to the door to say her master was not at home.

'Poppycock,' said the cabinet maker, pushing her aside. 'Don't stand there, girl, go and get him.'

The maid tried again. 'As I said, the mayor…'

'This won't take long,' said the cabinet maker who was a bottle short of sobriety.

The mayor's wife, hurried into the hall to see who was causing the fuss. She was a tall, striking woman, cleverer than her husband, and had been married to him long enough to be deeply disappointed by him. Unlike the other women in the village she wore modern dress and still after many years was regarded as a newcomer. Her only friend had been Edith's grandmother.

'Can I help you?' she said.

She was perplexed to see Edith was holding a bible.

'No,' said the cabinet maker. 'Women only complicate matters. I want to see the mayor.'

'Is it about the wedding?'

'Yes. And I want to see the mayor.'

Edith, her head bowed, wished she'd been able to tell Demetrius where she was going before she'd been dragged here. She knew there was something inherently wrong in what was being asked of her.

'I haven't congratulated you on your engagement,' said Georgeta to Edith.

Edith thanked her.

'You must be delighted,' said Georgeta to the cabinet maker.

'What, me?' said the cabinet maker. 'Why should I be delighted? Would you be pleased if your son married a gypsy?'

The question remained unanswered.

Impatiently, he looked round the hall, then, his words slipping together, he said, 'Edith must swear on her mother's bible.'

'Why? What must she swear?'

'Oh, you wouldn't understand.'

The commotion outside his study had woken the mayor from his afternoon sleep. He sat up, brushing his hair back. The mayor retained about him the shadow of the handsome young man who was used to having all he wanted without the inconvenience of trying. He enjoyed the idea of being mayor more than the work the role demanded of him, for he was lazy by nature, but he'd had the good fortune to marry a woman who wasn't.

'Tell them to come in,' he called into the hall.

'About time,' said the cabinet maker. He marched into the study and stood in front of the mayor's desk.

'What's all this about?' said the mayor. He looked at his wife who shrugged. He looked at Edith.

'I want you to witness Edith swearing that if the shepherd isn't back by first snowfall, she will marry the butcher.'

At the word 'butcher' the mayor's attitude changed. He sat up a little straighter, his expression became more serious. This Edith noted.

'I want it written down,' said her father, slapping the mayor's desk. 'On proper paper with the letters at the top, that you witnessed Edith's oath and what she swore to.' He swayed a little.

Georgeta put her hand lightly on Edith's arm.

'This isn't right,' she said to the mayor. 'How can it be? Edith is betrothed to the shepherd – her father consented. How can she now be contracted to the butcher? It's not... it's not moral.'

She threw the last word at her husband. He looked away from her and said, 'Thank you, Georgeta, you may go.'

As the cabinet maker began to tell the mayor all over again what was required, Georgeta whispered to Edith, 'You mustn't do this, my dear. You don't have to.'

'I have no choice,' Edith whispered back. 'But don't worry, Demetrius will be back for the harvest supper.'

'I hope so,' said Georgeta and kissed her cheek before she left the room.

\*

It wasn't from naivety that Edith complied but from a certainty that her love would be as true as the snow that fell every winter. Though she had to admit to a nagging voice inside her head that said, 'You are tempting fate.'

That evening she went to find Demetrius and they walked hand in hand down to the old forge. The air smelled of spring, of new beginnings. Tentatively, she told him what had happened.

He listened then said, 'What a foolish man the butcher must be. An old dog marking trees.' He stopped when he saw the worry in her smile and said, reassuringly, 'Nothing will come of it.'

How empty the word 'nothing' sounded to Edith. It was a word she knew all too well. Nothing had been her life before Demetrius had appeared.

'I'll be back,' he said. 'Don't be upset.'

'I shouldn't have sworn on my mother's bible.'

'It makes no difference, my love. If it's the only way your father will agree to our marriage, what does it matter? We'll be married well before the first snow.'

'It seems so long to wait until we can be together,' she said and kissed him hungrily.

He held her tight. 'We are together. No man can separate us.'

\*

The village being small and gossip cheap, and love a rare thing hardly ever seen, the neighbours' talk was all of Edith and her shepherd. They had been taken aback by how fast she had agreed to marry him, especially when they considered all the eligible suitors she had turned down. But the gossip that stayed on their lips and in their minds was the news that Edith had sworn on her dead mother's bible to marry the butcher if the shepherd didn't return by snowfall.

'No – never,' said Una, the butcher's daughter, when she heard.

'It's true,' said her sister, Vanda. 'The cabinet maker had the paper signed by the mayor and then he gave it to our father.'

'Never,' said Una again. 'It will never happen.'

# CHAPTER FOUR

## A DEAD LAMB'S FLEECE

Demetrius dreamed he was standing with Edith by the small stream beyond the orchard at the end of her garden. The sun was setting, and Edith was laughing as she criss-crossed the water. In her hand was a small bunch of snowdrops. He followed her and back and forth they went in the same rhythm until he realised that he was on the far side of the stream which was now a river. Edith called to him and each time she was further away until she was lost in the mist.

With a gasp Demetrius woke, drowning, into the dawn of a new day.

All that morning, the dream stubbornly stayed with him as he and his dog checked the flock. He rounded up the three ewes that hadn't yet given birth, and took into the pen a lamb whose mother had rejected it. Soon there would be no more excuses to stay. Tomorrow, the next day, he would take his flock up into the mountain. He was so lost in the dream of Edith that he was unaware of a well-built, compact young man standing a little way off, staring at him. Demetrius wondered why his dog hadn't barked.

'Good morning,' called Demetrius.

The young man didn't answer.

He continued with his work. One of the ewes was in trouble and gave birth to a dead lamb, bleating out her misery. He left the carcass on a bale of straw near where the abandoned lamb was penned. He was busy with another sheep when he saw the young man picking up the dead lamb.

Demetrius asked what he was doing but the young man didn't reply.

Strange, thought Demetrius, but he would have to deal with it later. It was only after he'd checked the other ewes that the young man reappeared, carrying the abandoned lamb. He'd covered it in the dead lamb's fleece.

Demetrius put the lamb in the pen with the bereaved ewe and they watched as she began to suckle it as if it were her own.

'Thank you,' said Demetrius. 'You did that very well. What's your name?'

He waited and he thought the lad might not have heard him so he repeated the question.

The young man, turning his head to one side, said, 'My name is Misha.'

'Can you hear?' Demetrius asked him.

'One ear only,' said Misha. His lack of hearing caused his words to come out slowly as if he was gathering his sentences together.

Demetrius held out his hand and invited Misha to share his breakfast. They sat down to eat the bread that Edith had baked for him, with cheese, honey and sweet tea.

'You're going to marry the cabinet maker's daughter,' said Misha.

'Yes,' said Demetrius.

'Good. And you will be back before snowfall.'

Demetrius laughed. 'Is there anyone in the village who hasn't heard about the oath?'

Misha didn't laugh. 'You must be back,' he said.

'I will be,' said Demetrius. And for a reason he didn't fully understand he told Misha about his dream, and the uneasy feeling it had left him with.

'You'll think me stupid,' he added.

'No,' said Misha. 'Stupid is my role, not yours. You're the stranger, the lover. I'm the idiot.'

Demetrius chose not to reply to that but said, 'I fear something might happen to Edith while I'm away. This is the first spring since becoming a shepherd that I wished I didn't have to leave.'

'I'll look out for her.'

'Thank you,' said Demetrius and wondered why he felt no better for having spoken about his fears.

The morning went well. Demetrius didn't ask Misha to help but he was happy to have some company and they worked hard until for no apparent reason his dog began to whine.

'Quiet,' said Demetrius.

Then, near the barn where the farmer allowed him to sleep, he saw a man, broad-shouldered, square-shaped. He was watching them.

Misha saw him too and all his confidence left him and it seemed to Demetrius that he shivered to the size of a child as the man approached. Demetrius calmed the dog, thinking there was something menacing about him.

'How long until you are gone, shepherd?' asked the man.

'A matter of days,' Demetrius replied.

The man turned to Misha. 'Tell your mother I want her to clean the house. If not her, then her sister.' Misha didn't move. 'Do you hear me, you half-wit?'

'No, he didn't,' said Demetrius. 'He's deaf in one ear.'

'And who are you to tell me what my grandson is?'

The word 'grandson' took Demetrius by surprise.

'This idiot,' said the man, grabbing Misha by the ear, 'is daft not deaf. Isn't that right?'

Misha twisted his whole body so he could hear his grandfather.

'Yes,' he said.

His grandfather let go of him. 'Tell this shepherd what I don't like.'

Demetrius could see Misha concentrating on every word and piecing them together.

'I don't like...' the man repeated.

'Strangers,' said Misha, keeping his eyes on the ground. He knew what was coming, there was no need to read his grandfather's lips.

'I don't like…'

'Gypsies.'

'I don't like… tell him,' said the man and he clipped his grandson across the head. 'Tell him!'

'Village girls marrying strangers.'

'Out of the mouth of an idiot comes the truth. The sooner you leave, shepherd, the better.' As he strolled away he shouted to Misha, 'Don't forget to tell your mother.'

When he'd gone Misha picked up his coat.

'Please – stay a while,' said Demetrius. 'You've been more than helpful.'

'I hate him,' muttered Misha. 'I hate him. He ruins everything.'

'You're not an idiot,' said Demetrius. 'You're deaf in one ear.'

'In this village, I'm an idiot. Born stupid, nothing in my brain, and whatever anyone tells me falls out, forgotten, the second it has gone in. I will instantly forget what he asked me to do. My mother won't clean his house, anyway. I work for the blacksmith, but he's wary of me because of my grandfather.'

'Why? Who is he?' asked Demetrius.

'He's the butcher.'

The word hit Demetrius so hard that he felt it as a physical blow, taking his breath away.

'The butcher?' he said, stunned.

He had been a fool. He should have realised the implications when Edith told him of the promise she'd made but he'd seen it as a simple piece of nonsense. Now he felt a cold dread and the image of Edith alone on the other side of the river came back to him.

Misha said, quietly, 'I'm sorry, I was stupid, I should've…'

Demetrius put a hand on his shoulder. 'You are far from stupid. I'm the idiot, not you. I have to leave…' He stopped, seeing the anxiety on Misha's face. 'Can you read?' he asked.

'Yes, Edith taught me. I have one book – of fairy tales.'

Demetrius opened his rucksack.

'Here,' he said. 'It's a book I like and you might too. It's about a man in the time of the Thirty Years' War who everyone thinks is a simpleton. He isn't.'

Misha took the book, an expression of genuine wonder on his face.

'You'll lend this book to me?'

'No, it's yours to keep.'

'That makes two books. I'm a king of two books,' he laughed. 'Thank you.'

Demetrius noticed that he carefully hid the book in his coat.

# CHAPTER FIVE

## FROM THE ONE

By the time Demetrius and Misha said goodbye, it had started to rain. The farm was a fair walk from the village and below Demetrius could see the houses huddled together, smoke coming from the chimneys. From a distance it looked as if it belonged in a children's book. Yet nothing was that simple, except his love for Edith. She had become the reason for everything. The moment he first saw her he knew he'd waited perhaps many lifetimes to find her. As he neared the cabinet maker's house, the feeling of apprehension in him grew. He had hardly thought about the butcher before, but now he knew him to be a cruel man of sharp edges and granite determination. And the thought came to him, as heavy as thunder, too terrible to contemplate, that the dream was a warning.

'No,' he said aloud, almost shaking himself. 'That will never happen.'

He cursed himself for judging the butcher to be unimportant.

The rain was dancing in the puddles as he opened the gate to the yard. The hens had taken cover under the verandah, as had the pig. Demetrius pushed it aside and stood in the doorway.

The cabinet maker was ranting.

'And when do I have time for that? You expect me to work all day and then come home and mend the house?'

'Other men do,' said Edith and muttered something that Demetrius didn't catch.

'What?' said her father. 'What did you say?'

Edith put down a bucket and straightened herself.

'I said, if you were sober you could earn the money to repair the roof.'

'Not another word from you, girl,' said the cabinet maker, lifting his hand.

Demetrius caught it before it struck Edith. Her father tried to free himself but with one swift movement Demetrius had him seated in a chair.

The cabinet maker was so surprised that for a moment he was quiet.

'I've come to mend the roof,' said Demetrius.

'Go away,' shouted the cabinet maker. 'I regret that I ever...' he stopped.

Demetrius never took his light blue eyes off him.

He waited until all the anger was gone, then said, 'You will help me.'

Edith watched, incredulous, as her father followed Demetrius like a lamb and went to work. By the time the rain had stopped that evening the roof leaked no more.

'How did you do that?' Edith asked Demetrius after the supper plates were cleared away and the cabinet maker had retired to the inn.

'I don't know, but it works with sheep. It's a knack that will be useful when dealing with your father after we're married.'

\*

Demetrius decided not to tell her about the butcher's visit. Not that evening for it was their last until he returned. He played the violin as he had many nights and willed his soul to never leave hers. He felt that he had lived in shadows and only now in her silent gaze of love was there light.

'What are you thinking?' he asked Edith as he put his violin away.

What she had been thinking was that he was the first person, apart from her grandmother, who had ever valued her, ever seen her for herself. But she didn't say that.

What she said was, 'Why do you love me? I have no worth in this village, I have no dowry.'

'I knew when I first saw you that all that I would be, and all that I could be, lay with you,' he said.

'I feel the same,' said Edith. 'You are the clearing in the forest, a place of safety.'

'Why a clearing in a forest?' he asked.

'My grandmother used to say the forest is the darkest place we know. We imagine it to be full of wolves, bears and the bloodless. There we hope to find the storyteller's cabin, a place of safety, and to pick the berries that are redder than a red rose. I think love lies in the same forest and is no less hard to find.'

'Then we're blessed,' he said.

They talked into the night, his lips gentle on her cheek as he whispered words of love. Their fingers entwined, they leaned closer together until they could feel the warmth of the other's body.

The cabinet maker staggered into the yard that night cursing moon and man. He didn't see them as two people. He saw them as one and was thrown when from the one Demetrius stood up.

'Go home,' shouted the cabinet maker. 'Go home.'

The following morning Edith went out before dawn, still in her nightdress, in the hope that she might stop the time from gathering hours. She walked down to the orchard to where the stream ran and the air smelled of lilac blossom. She sat holding her knees as the world changed colour and the ducks laughed at the light of the new day.

Then she saw him and his little dog in the sunlight and for a moment it seemed that he was on the other side of a great river, not a stream. She stood up and, not minding her bare feet, she ran to him.

'I'll be back for the harvest supper,' he said. He took her

hand and kissed her palm. 'Remember, I will love you always. Nothing – not even death – will change that.'

With unbearable sadness she watched as his flock, their bells jingling, made their way up the mountain to the green pastures.

# CHAPTER SIX

## WHO HAS LOST IT EVER GRIEVES

Edith told herself spring would soon pass and summer would tumble into autumn and Demetrius would return. Perhaps, this time next year, they would be expecting a baby, a new voice to echo in the mountains. These thoughts in their simplicity comforted her.

She remembered her grandmother's stories about a pair of boots that could stride up mountains as if they were molehills, that could stand in lakes and think them puddles. If only she had such a pair of boots, she thought, she would be gone from this place, from her drunken father. She would climb the mountain, she would find Demetrius and stay with him. She felt the longing in every bone and muscle – but she didn't leave. She and Demetrius would never be accepted as a married couple if it was known she'd run after her lover. She must be patient. In her dreams she nightly found him under a different moon.

The sun became hotter; the grass dried yellow, scattered with poppies. The swallows ruled the sky and the village streets became dusty. Edith's skin turned brown. Her garden grew, as did her corn. All the days were the same, as if time, made soporific by the sun, had forgotten to move the hands of the clock. In the evening she would sit on the verandah sewing Demetrius' red shirt, her eyes on the mountain, noting every passing hour. He would have taken his flock high up where the wind was cool and where there were fewer flies to bother the sheep. Amid the green grass, the young lambs would grow strong legs, ready to be sold in the harvest markets. She counted the days until the shepherd's return. Never once did she doubt him or his love of her.

She saw her marriage as a new beginning, an escape from her father, a man who had never cherished her. With Demetrius, there was a chance to start again with a clean piece of cloth on which a different future could be embroidered.

The remoteness of the village meant there were few visitors, even in the summer months. No one ventured that far up the mountain and only the men of the village ever went down to the town to bring back salt, sugar, things that couldn't be made or grown on the land.

One day a hunting party arrived at the inn. It was ill-prepared for such a large, raucous group of guests. The huntsmen required rooms, wine and food and drank late into the night, throwing the small inn into chaos. The innkeeper had to ask for help from the village women so the guest rooms could be aired and cleaned. An incident occurred and the innkeeper called upon the mayor to lay down the law.

'What happened?' asked Edith.

'Nothing,' said her father, swaying. 'Just a piece of harmless fun. And anyway, Sorina enjoyed it.'

Sorina was the butcher's granddaughter.

'She is fifteen. What harmless fun?' asked Edith.

'You'd know if you were married.'

'How many huntsmen are there?' she asked.

'Four or five.'

'Have you seen them?'

'Seen them, talked to them. They want a guide.'

'Guide to where?' asked Edith.

'Up the mountain,' said the cabinet maker. 'They're wealthy merchants – by the look of them they've never done a day's hard work in their lives. Only used to the weight of a pen. They don't wear boots. Who wears shoes to climb a mountain?'

'What are they hunting?' asked Edith.

'Bear,' said her father, 'and pretty young girls.' He roared with laughter. 'One of them wants to go high into the mountain. The butcher offered to take him.'

That was all the sense she could make of her father's ramblings.

Edith didn't give the hunting party another thought. Neither did she see them on their way back down the mountain. They stayed one more night at the inn, complaining that the weather had been against them and they'd had no luck with the bear.

'Sorina is smitten by one of the young men,' or so the cabinet maker said.

Edith thought, what could he know of love?

\*

Summer began to fade. The heat lingered but the nights had a slight chill to them. The red shirt was finished and in a matter of days it would be the harvest supper.

'I don't believe he's coming back,' said Edith's father one night.

'What makes you say that?'

'I've been thinking – why would he want you? You'd bring him nothing, no dowry, nothing.'

'He will be back,' said Edith.

The cabinet maker threw up his arms. 'All I'm saying is perhaps...' He lost his balance and sat down abruptly. 'Perhaps you should think of the chickens you have in the yard instead of dreaming of the cockerel you'll never own.'

'Where did you find that pearl of wisdom?'

'It's just that the butcher...'

The butcher. Edith shuddered. She felt as if someone was standing on her grave.

She stood up straight and said, 'I'm betrothed to Demetrius, and it is he who I will marry.'

'If he comes back,' said her father. 'Personally, I think he would be a fool to come here again. What have you to offer him? Just some pretty stitches on a red shirt.'

'He will be here,' said Edith.

The promise to the butcher – or rather the idea that the promise might not be kept – now worried the cabinet maker. And being a man without the ability to keep his worries to himself, he imprudently confessed them to the butcher. But the butcher seemed remarkably unconcerned.

'There was no betrothal supper, was there?' the butcher asked, and before the cabinet maker could think of a coherent answer, he continued, 'If there was one I don't remember being invited nor were the other village elders. I ask myself, what kind of wedding would it be without keeping the traditions of this village?'

'You're right,' said the cabinet maker. 'But what if…'

'Go home,' said the butcher, 'and don't worry yourself needlessly. If he comes back, then he comes back.'

Yes, thought the cabinet maker, if the shepherd returns I will tell him, God be my witness, that he can't marry Edith. A bottle of plum brandy was enough for him to turn a shepherd into a lamb.

The next day, a cartload of logs for the winter arrived at the cabinet maker's yard, and the sight of them gave the old drunk hope.

'What other deal have you done with the butcher?' asked Edith.

It wasn't a word of a lie when her father said, 'None that I know of,' and, tucking a bottle of plum brandy under his arm, went off to his bed.

'Wait,' said Edith. 'Where did that come from?'

'What? Now can't a man have a drink in his own house?'
Edith had misjudged his sobriety. He caught hold of her.
'You will marry the butcher, do you hear me, girl?' he said
and struck her across the face. 'You will marry the butcher.'

\*

Edith felt she'd waited an eternity for this day. Her face still
bore the faint mark of a bluish bruise but it didn't matter.
She had spent the past week thinking what she was going
to wear. Now, at last, the day was here. Dressed in her
finest petticoat, her second-best embroidered skirt and with
flowers laced in her hair, she joined the women of the village
to cook the harvest supper.

Edith could hardly think of anything except Demetrius
coming home to her. She was lost in a daydream when the
miller's wife took her aside and told her she was lucky that
the butcher was willing to wait so long for her.

'He can wait as long as he likes,' said Edith. 'I won't be
marrying him.'

'I heard you made a promise,' said the miller's wife, 'in
front of the mayor.'

'I made a promise to Demetrius, and it is he who I'm
marrying,' said Edith. 'He'll be back tonight – you'll see.'

Edith had never much liked the miller's wife or the miller's
son who had married her best friend. Lena's mother, a widow,
had given her no choice but to marry a suitor chosen for
her by the village elders. Lena was twenty, the same age as

Edith, and now there was a sharpness about her that hadn't been there before.

'Edith,' Lena said, 'do you honestly think your shepherd, with his midnight looks, gives any thought to you? I doubt it. I imagine that wherever he plays his violin, there's a girl waiting.'

'You're just jealous because I'm marrying a man I love, not someone the elders say I should marry.'

'It's tradition,' said Lena. 'To make sure we keep outsiders out.'

'Perhaps we should welcome a few more in.'

The butcher's granddaughter, Sorina, teased her. 'Did his kisses taste of strawberries? Did he steal your gold coin?'

'Don't be so silly,' said Edith. 'You're far too young to know what you're talking about. Now go and help with the cooking.'

'Grandpa said you'll be marrying him,' she said.

'Your grandpa is wrong because I won't,' said Edith.

Three times that day, she saw Demetrius, felt his hand on her shoulder, spun round to find nothing there but wind and shadow.

The night came. The full moon stared down on the small village nestling in the arms of the mountain, the church at its centre surrounded by fortified walls, the houses close together in their gabled splendour, all brightly painted, each with an inscription rendered in neat lettering. The verse on the cabinet maker's house read:

\*

*Tell me for what gold is fit?*
*Who has got none longs for it.*
*Who has got it, fears for thieves.*
*Who has lost it ever grieves.*

\*

A truth Edith's father had never heeded.

The bells rang out into the mountain, and the women sang, as they had for centuries, to call the men in from the fields. The long table in the middle of the village hall was covered in an embroidered cloth, jugs of wine, painted plates piled high with food. One by one the men entered, took off their hats and took their places at the table, until there was only one empty seat: that of the shepherd.

And a whisper like a late summer wasp went round the hall. 'If he doesn't come back soon, Edith will have to marry the butcher.'

His two stiff, matronly daughters looked on, disapproving.

Edith didn't eat. She stared at the door, willing the shepherd to appear even at this late hour, willing him so hard that if dust could gather itself together she would have conjured him from its particles. After the plates were cleared, the band began to play, and the lads and lasses took their positions on the dance floor. Edith stood motionless, not daring to move. If not today, then tomorrow. Yes, he will be here tomorrow.

'Where's your shepherd then?' It was the butcher.

Edith held herself straight. 'Tomorrow,' she said. 'He will be back tomorrow.'

'I doubt it,' said the butcher.

With his words echoing in her ears, Edith helped her father to their door.

# CHAPTER SEVEN

## THE ROOT OF HER TONGUE

Tomorrow came and there was no sign of Demetrius, nor was there the day after. Edith went over everything that could have happened to him, until dread flooded through her. She asked the shepherds who had been at the harvest supper if they had seen him and none of them had.

With every passing day, her father's mood improved. The wind began to blow in autumn; the leaves, skittish in their falling, heralded the snow to come.

'The days are getting shorter. Soon it will be winter,' he said, rubbing his hands together, glad he'd had the foresight to make Edith swear the oath in the mayor's office. 'Demetrius – if that is his name – probably stole the sheep and took them to the next village. I know many a farmer who would have bought them. What do you say to that, girl? He's off somewhere else – back to his wife.'

Still, be still, Edith told her worried mind. He will come back; you must believe it, you know it in your heart. He'll be here before the first snowflake touches the ground. You must believe it.

And another day passed and only now did she wonder why she'd never asked where he had come from. It was the simplest of questions. It seemed at the time unimportant for the cords that bound them wouldn't be broken. But there was no one to ask. She didn't even know his family name. He had told her he came from a town, that he had been educated; but in which city, he never said. He loved gypsy music and the outdoor life, and that had led him to become a shepherd, to learn the old ways. He'd told her that her grandmother was famous, that her stories had travelled far. Travelled where? She should have asked Demetrius so many questions and hadn't, believing they would have a lifetime for answers. She had no answers.

Panic engulfed her. What if he'd had an accident? How would anyone know? The village elders must send a search party to find him. She dreaded asking them but she had no choice.

The head of the elders was the butcher and she was relieved he was standing behind his colleagues while she begged them to find Demetrius.

'No,' was their firm answer. 'He is not from this village, not from this mountain. He knows little about our ways; he is not one of us.'

'I am betrothed to him.'

'Who says so?' they asked.

'My father gave his consent.'

'He didn't ask our permission. Were rings exchanged? Was there a betrothal supper?'

'No, but none of that matters. We are engaged.'

It was as if a wall was falling on her brick by brick, all hope being buried. Why wouldn't they help? The answer was simple. She could see it in the butcher's hand.

He showed the elders the piece of paper Edith had signed.

'No,' they said again. 'We will not search for the shepherd.'

Shaking with rage, Edith let out a howl of pain. It came from deep inside her, it rose to fill the room, loud enough to wake the mountain giant.

'Silence,' said the elders. 'Such a noise is unseemly. Perhaps we should set a date for the wedding.'

'No!' cried Edith.

'Not another word, woman.'

'I can wait until the snow comes,' said the butcher magnanimously. 'After all, that was the promise.'

'There will be no wedding,' said Edith.

There was nothing more she could do. Only too aware of her powerlessness, she walked home with the elders' word ringing in her ears, through her whole body. Silence. And she felt that the root of her tongue had begun to wither.

'It's what women do: bear sorrow quietly,' she said to herself. 'All our grief we keep hidden in empty wombs.'

She would go down to the stream in the evenings and look up at the mountain, hoping, praying that Demetrius would appear.

'You know what happens to maidens who stay out after dark,' her father would shout. 'The bloodless come for them.'

Each day that autumn, she felt her words fall away. The cabinet maker, taking no notice, became more indebted to the butcher. She had tried to argue with her father but it was hopeless.

'The butcher will destroy us if we don't pay him back.'

She noticed as she said it that the words weighed heavy on her tongue. It had become difficult to speak.

'But I will pay him back.' A lie, another lie. Her father's words corrupted by deceit. 'The debts are cancelled the minute you marry him,' said her father.

He was pleased to see the yard filled with logs and his cellar filled with wine, hams hanging in the kitchen and apples stored for the winter. And, better still, no sign of the shepherd.

*

The mornings were thick with frost and the air smelled of snow. Every day Edith found the effort to talk harder. The walnut tree in the yard was losing its leaves just as she was losing her words. They fell from her one by one.

She had to do her household chores, to listen to her father gloating. Even her friends seemed to take delight in Demetrius' absence.

The women were gathered at the miller's house when the first snow fell. Edith stopped her work and looked out of the window at the sky. She didn't realise she was crying.

'I told you so. It's your grandmother's doing that you believe those fairy stories,' Lena said. 'But no golden prince is coming to save you from your promise. Perhaps he makes a habit of wooing young women.'

Edith knew she no longer possessed enough words to quarrel with her friend. They were buried inside her, lying under the root of her tongue. The ill-advised oath was going to seal her fate. She thought of leaving the village but who in the town would employ a village girl? And what if Demetrius returned and found her gone?

She couldn't sleep. When her father was in bed she would wander round the house, haunted by a vision of Demetrius lying dead in a crevasse, his violin case by his side, his raggle-taggle dog gone. How did she know?

'Some people see what others can't,' her grandmother had told her. 'You are one of those.'

One night Edith seemed to see her grandmother's ghost sitting by the kitchen fire, rocking back and forth.

'Where is he?' she wordlessly asked the ghost.

'Dead,' crackled the fire. 'The violin by his side and your gold coin in his hand.'

When the first snow covered the village in its velvet blanket, Edith was silent. She had no more words in her to whisper against her teeth. Overnight her hair turned white. Speechless, she held the weight of his loss in her soul.

# CHAPTER EIGHT

## THE WEDDING GOWN

The cabinet maker let out a cry when he saw her. Genuinely frightened, his hands shook as he poured himself a glass of plum brandy.

'What have you done?' he said. Edith didn't reply. 'If you think this will stop the marriage, remember – you gave your word on your mother's bible.' Emboldened by the brandy, he shouted at her, banging his fist on the table. 'Tell me – what have you done?'

Still Edith said nothing. There being no mirror for her to gaze in, it didn't matter if her hair was black or white though she took some pleasure in the look of horror on her father's face.

'Speak,' he shouted.

But Edith couldn't speak. She'd woken that morning, her mouth a hollow cave, empty of sound. She watched her father, his arms flailing, and realised for the first time that this silence was a room she could live in. No one speaks to a closed door. There are two parts to a conversation.

'Do you hear me?'

No, she thought. Because I don't want to. You can argue with yourself. Perhaps that's who you've been arguing with all your life. She didn't try to stop him when he poured another glass, his face contorted, his breath stale as he came close to her. Had she ever loved him, she wondered. She'd loved her grandmother.

Her grandmother had told her, 'If you don't like the story you are telling yourself, make up a different one and change the ending.'

Edith had tried to change the ending to her father's story. Now she didn't care. The only way to endure the rest of her life without Demetrius was to tell herself stories. Stories would be the furnishings of her silent room.

Her father's jaws moved up and down; he had an ugly set of teeth. She was surprised at how easy it was to let go of another person's words. They became a jumble of sound, a mass of cockroaches, click-clicking, all marching in the same direction.

'Your feet have always dangled above the earth,' he yelled. 'You've been like that since the day you were born. You will marry the butcher.'

\*

*Demetrius, my love, when the ground has become too hard, when winter has crept into this house, when the darkness begins to fill the cracks with the ghost of a summer past, you will be in my heart, a snow song away. Never leave me.*

\*

The cabinet maker didn't know what to make of this silent, white-haired daughter. She seemed not to care what he said to her, never showed any expression.

His mind fragmented by drink, he feared that Demetrius had become one of the bloodless. Hadn't he sucked Edith's voice from her? It would explain the paleness of her skin, her white hair. In fear of an attack, the cabinet maker started to wear his shirt inside out.

He was anxious that the butcher might think it unlucky to have a wife with white hair who stared at you instead of speaking. What worried him more was that his daughter might not keep her promise. Promises, as he knew all too well, were easily broken. He couldn't remember how many times he had made a promise to stop drinking and not one of them had he kept. His excuse was that the devil was in the bottle. No matter what he did, the moment the cork was pulled, the devil came calling with no regard for the time of day. But surely a promise sworn on a bible in front of the mayor was a different matter? You couldn't break that without holy consequences.

He told the butcher about Edith's hair and her silence. He kept his thoughts about the bloodless to himself.

'I have two daughters,' said the butcher. 'They have more than enough to say. Why would I need a talkative wife?'

The butcher thought back to when Edith had pleaded with the elders for help. Silence was what they'd demanded of her.

'It'll pass,' he said and sent the cabinet maker home.

When the villagers heard that a wedding date had been set, there was a collective sigh of relief.

Still, the butcher wanted to be sure that her white hair had not detracted from her beauty. Dressed in his Sunday best, he called on Edith, taking with him two rabbits he'd shot. Seeing her made him certain that he was the luckiest of men. He placed his offerings on the kitchen table and sat opposite her. She didn't move. She caught his stare. Not once did she lower her eyes as she used to.

Edith told herself, don't look away. She watched as the butcher, not knowing where to rest his eyes under her bright gaze, studied his hat and, for the first time, felt his hands to be too big, his shoes to be too heavy. Embarrassed, he could only steal a look at her.

He said, 'The wedding will take place in a month's time. What do you say to that?'

Silence.

'I've decided to have a wedding dress made for you – the kind that the grand women in the town wear. I can well afford it. Would you like that?'

Not a word. Not a change in her expression.

Twisting his hat in his hand he said, 'I'm not a bad man.' He dared to glance at her again as he said it. 'I'm sure you've heard talk. Unfounded talk. My late wife, unlike you, she never stopped with her words. Never a day of peace, made up of complaints. You met her.'

Edith knew her silence to be her only protection, an impenetrable shield against him. She listened as he went against the grain of all he believed with the promise of a wedding dress. Did he think that was enough to buy him her consent? A way to appease his conscience? What role, Edith wondered, had he played in Demetrius' disappearance? She didn't doubt that he had something to do with it.

Her silence rattled the butcher. He was used to noise, the squeals of dying animals, his daughters bickering, his granddaughter arguing. But in this thick silence he could hear his own unanswered questions.

'Should have shaved better,' he said as he ran his hand over his chin. There was not another sound to disturb the peace. The butcher cleared his throat. He told himself Edith would come round to the idea of being married. He was doing a good thing. It was simple: her father was a drunkard; she needed a husband and, although he was old enough to be her father, he was also the most powerful man in the village.

'Good,' he said standing, hitting his hat on his legs. 'That's agreed. I'll ask the seamstress to visit you.'

The cabinet maker was waiting on the verandah.

'Everything all right?' he asked.

The butcher was startled to hear someone speak.

'Yes,' he said. 'Give me a silent woman any day.'

Her father told Edith she should be grateful that an upstanding man was prepared to marry her.

'There was gossip after you were born. People said your mother must have brought you back from the goblin market. Quiet!' he shouted at the silence between them. 'I need some peace.'

And taking his pipe he went to his room to drink his brandy.

Edith held to the memory of her shepherd. Their future was gone and only a dark forest stood waiting. Her loss of speech and the loss of her lover were as one; her grief a leaden sadness. A month, just a month, and she would be married to the butcher whose hands smelled of blood.

# CHAPTER NINE

## A PRETTY PENNY

Every spring, just after the snow had melted, the seamstress would say farewell to her brother the blacksmith, leave the village and make the long journey into the nearest town. There she would stay in rooms rented from the Schmidts. She would wear her own gowns and make dresses for wealthy ladies who pored over French fashion plates and wanted nothing to do with the traditional costumes of the region. In the winter, before the heavy snow set in and made the roads impassable, she would return to the village, content to abide by its customs, its strict rules regarding clothes, and never talk about what she did for a living.

This time she brought home with her a brand-new sewing machine. It was this that had made her business more successful than ever before. For the first time she had enough orders to keep her employed through the winter months and enough money to buy her brother a present: a cuckoo clock.

The blacksmith looked at it, amazed. He had never seen one before.

'Does it work?' he asked.

'Yes,' said Flora, laughing.

Her brother held it as if it were made of glass rather than wood and with great care hung it on the kitchen wall. His face lit up like that of a child when the wooden bird cuckooed. Such a strange noise, Flora thought, to hear at this quiet hour. The blacksmith sat at the kitchen table, mesmerised by the clock. Almost in a whisper, as if words might frighten the wooden bird away, he said, 'I've cooked a meal for us.'

Flora smiled to herself. She was always impressed by how tidy and clean her brother kept the house. She said she was going to change her clothes, adding, 'I've so much to tell you.'

He caught her hand and brought it to his lips. 'I've missed you,' he said. 'Stand in the light a moment.' Flora moved to the fire. The blacksmith said, almost to himself, 'You look beautiful.' And then his face clouded. 'Is there enough money? You bought a sewing machine and a cuckoo clock.'

'I wouldn't have done if there hadn't been enough,' she said and took a fat package from her bag and put it on the kitchen table.

'What would I do without you?' said the blacksmith.

\*

They were having breakfast the following morning when Flora looked up and in the gloom of the new day saw the butcher standing in the middle of their yard.

'What's he doing here?' asked Flora.

'I should have told you last night,' said her brother. 'But with the cuckoo clock and all, I forgot.'

There was a knock on the kitchen door and the butcher came in.

'Good morning,' he said. He looked at Flora. 'You're back?'

There was little point in answering such a foolish question.

'That's as it should be,' said the butcher.

She had never liked this man. He was crude and a bully. Her brother's face remained expressionless. Reluctantly she offered the butcher a cup of coffee.

'I can't stay. I've come to ask you to go and see Edith.'

'Edith?' repeated Flora. It seemed a strange request. She couldn't think why he would want her to visit Edith.

'I'm going to see her today,' said Flora.

The butcher looked awkward and went to study the cuckoo clock.

'Does it make a noise?' he asked.

'It does,' said the blacksmith.

'Must have cost a pretty penny,' said the butcher, 'for some bits of carved wood.'

The fact that Flora earned a living and wasn't dependent upon a man was one of the reasons she was looked on in the village with suspicion. The other reason was that she wasn't married and no one could see a rhyme or reason to that one.

'I had hoped to be back in time for her wedding,' said Flora. 'I'm sorry to have missed it. She's been much on my mind.'

'When does it make the noise?' asked the butcher.

'It makes a soft noise on the half hour and on the quarter, and then a full-blown cuckoo on the hour,' said the blacksmith.

'Then there are four minutes until I hear it,' said the butcher.

Flora put down her coffee cup and was going to excuse herself when the butcher said, 'It's not yet.' She couldn't think what he was referring to. 'You haven't missed it.'

Flora looked at her brother who shrugged.

'Edith's marriage to Demetrius?' she said.

'No,' said the butcher. 'The shepherd never came back to the village. He probably went off and married another girl.'

Flora stared at him incredulously. 'What makes you think that?' she said. 'Did anyone go looking for him when he failed to return?'

'What?' said the butcher. 'Pull him back by the scruff of his neck like a dog and make him marry Edith?'

Flora felt herself bristling with anger. 'There would be no making him – or Edith for that matter – do…' She stopped. The butcher's eyes were hard.

'Edith is marrying me,' he said. 'I've told her she can be married in a wedding dress, the kind you make for those fancy ladies down there in the town.'

'You?' she said. 'She is to marry you?'

The news was so shocking that she hardly knew what to say. 'Edith… Edith has agreed?'

The butcher ignored the question and said, 'A white wedding dress to match her hair.'

'Edith's hair is black,' said Flora.

'It turned white on the night she stopped talking,' said the butcher.

Flora was about to speak when the butcher put up his hand to stop her.

'Enough. No more questions. She is to have a white wedding dress. You are to make it.'

'I can't,' said Flora. 'It's forbidden by the village elders. You of all people know that. No one from here has ever been married in anything other than the traditional costume. The flax grown in the fields, spun here on the spinning wheels, the cloth woven, cut and stitched by hand. Edith showed me the skirt and blouse that she was going to be married in. Why would she want a modern wedding gown?'

The question hung as heavy as the snow-filled sky.

*Cuckoo. Cuckoo.*

'It makes a loud noise,' said the butcher. 'She is to have this dress. I will pay well for it, pay your fancy price.' He put up his collar and left, closing the yard gate behind him.

'Did you know about this?' said Flora, turning to her brother.

The blacksmith nodded. 'The whole village knows. When the shepherd didn't return, Edith lost the power of speech and her hair went white overnight. Everyone says the butcher is bewitched and that the wedding dress is Edith's doing.'

'You should have told me. Do you know what happened to the shepherd?'

Her brother sighed. 'I went up the mountain with Misha.'

'The butcher's grandson?' said Flora.

'He's been helping me.'

'I thought he was a fool,' said Flora. 'Are you sure it's wise?'

'He's a good worker. No one takes the time to listen to him. But if you don't fluster him, shout at him or raise your fist, he works hard.'

'And no doubt rushes back and tells his grandfather all that goes on here.'

'No,' said the blacksmith. 'He loves Edith and because she wants to know what happened to the shepherd, Misha searches the mountain in hope of finding him. He tells me he's listening for his violin. It was Misha who found the remains of the shepherd's dog and several of the sheep. They'd strayed far too high. We rounded up the rest of the flock and took them down to the farmer. There was no sign of the shepherd. The farmer told us that Demetrius would never have abandoned his animals.'

'This is wrong.'

'I know. But what can we do? We thought it best not to tell anyone. Edith hasn't said a word since the snow came. She listens but she doesn't speak.'

'She can't marry the butcher,' said Flora. 'He's as old as her father. And a brute.'

'We can't stop it,' said her brother. 'I'm one of the few men round here who doesn't owe the butcher – thanks to you. What he wants, he gets. And Flora, you must be careful when you go to confession. The priest isn't to be trusted – he and the butcher are as thick as thieves.'

She nodded. 'And what about the wedding gown? What do I do?'

'I don't know.'

# CHAPTER TEN

## THE ANGEL OF THE HOUSE

Edith sat in the neat kitchen with its large scrubbed table, bread baking in the oven. She stared at the blue jug that her grandmother would leave out every evening filled with water. She would say it was for the angel of the house. Often as a child, Edith had woken at night certain that she saw the angel, tall and growing taller, casting a shadow over her bed.

Her grandmother had taken these dreams seriously.

'What would happen if we didn't leave the jug out?' Edith had asked when she was a little older and more able to make sense of things unseen.

Grandmother said that if that was to happen, the evil one could make its way into the walls of the house. Edith thought now the only thing that had made its way into these walls was a deep sadness, a damp melancholy that refused to be defeated by the warmth of the stove. Her grandmother knew the mountain was rife with stories of the bloodless. The dread of the unknown was a bindweed of superstition that tied women to the house for fear of what might lie beyond the garden gate.

She would start her stories with 'What once took place and if it had never been it would not be told'.

Once, I loved a shepherd with eyes as blue as a winter sky. He was no prince, but to me, he was a king of men. What is this life without him, a life without hope? What is life without hope? A newly dug grave. Edith wiped her eyes with the back of her hand, swallowed her wordless misery. It tasted bitter. But life went on, not caring that she was broken. She still had to clean out the pigsty and feed the pig and the chickens. Her father still demanded his supper. It mattered not that her dreams had vanished.

Edith's white hair and her silence were of great interest to the villagers. No one said they were sorry or asked about Demetrius; it was as if he had never been there. The only person to enquire was the cobbler's wife, Vanda, and she, being also the butcher's daughter, had already made it quite clear that she didn't want a stepmother, certainly not one as young as Edith.

Edith had no intention of being married to an old man. Her father had sucked enough of her life from her. What can I do, she asked her heart, when you are broken, when I can't even speak in my defence? Her tongue sat unmoving, redundant in her mouth. An image of the butcher's slab came to her: the sheep's head, its tongue lolling out of its jaws.

At night she dreamed of Demetrius. She saw him floating over the village, his violin resting on his chest. He reached down towards her, their fingertips nearly touching. She felt his spirit enter her, run free through her blood – and then he was gone. In all her dreams he never spoke.

One morning, caring little for the superstition that had turned a water jug into a charm against evil, Edith picked it up, drank from it then went about her work. Later, as she refilled it from the well in the yard, she began to hear Demetrius in her head, speaking in a language without words. A language she understood.

*'The dead are meant to be silent, not the living, not you, my love.'*

Edith spoke to him in the same way.

*'Why can't I see you? Why in dreams do you have a shape and no voice? I hardly knew you and you're gone.'*

*'I'm here.'*

She watched the sunlight flickering on the surface of the blue jug.

*'How do I live knowing I've lost you, and years, meaningless years, spread out before me? I'm to be buried alive, a house my coffin, a wedding ring my chain, a white dress my shroud.'*

The sound of the gate made her jump. The seamstress was brushing her boots and the hem of her dress free of the snow. She came into the kitchen, put down her basket and gathered Edith to her.

'What has happened?' Flora asked. 'You look so pale – and your hair…'

There was only silence.

Edith was pleased to see Flora and at the same time dreaded the questions she would ask.

'Speak to me, Edith. I don't believe you can't talk. Has a doctor seen you?' Edith shook her head. 'You'd think we were living in the Middle Ages. Next year a train will run from the capital to the town and then this village will not be so isolated.'

Edith put the kettle on the stove and thought she should have left in the summer, gone up the mountain, found Demetrius and not cared what anyone thought. Now it was too late. Regret rubbed her raw. She took the bread from the oven. Better to be doing something, anything, rather than sit across from Flora. She patted the loaf out of the tin and sat it on the rack. The smell of the warm bread filled the kitchen.

'Please speak, Edith,' said Flora. 'I won't tell a soul if you do, I promise. I'm older than you by seven years and wise enough to see that your silence has a power of its own.'

Edith wished Flora would leave.

'The butcher came this morning talking nonsense about a wedding gown.'

Why do people speak so much, thought Edith, watching Flora busy herself with her basket.

*'Perhaps because the dead can't speak.'*

*'I think you might be right.'*

'Edith – are you listening?' said Flora. 'You should see a doctor in town. I know a good one.'

The idea that there was money to see the village doctor, let alone a doctor in town, nearly made Edith laugh. She put butter and jam on the table and gestured to Flora to help herself. She poured the tea, not listening. So many women live lives crushed by words.

'Edith?'

She looked up at Flora.

'Do you hear what I'm saying?'

No, because it brings me no comfort and, for me, unlike you, there's no escape. What is it like to live in town and make enough to support yourself? The priest says that 'seamstress' is just another word for 'prostitute'. I don't think that's your story. But there's something – something hidden.

'Was it your idea – the wedding dress?'

Edith shook her head.

'Then it was the butcher's. But why?' said Flora. 'Can't you convince him that you don't want it?'

Edith shook her head again.

It was then that Edith understood something about silence. And she began to listen to every word Flora said. She was right – the butcher should have known better than to suggest a modern wedding dress. Edith hadn't thought how much of a rebellious act against the old ways such a dress would be.

'People are talking. They say you've bewitched the butcher. They say Demetrius was a gypsy.'

Flora picked up her tape measure with a sigh. She took from her basket a folder of fashion plates, fine ladies with impossible shapes wearing wedding gowns. 'White is all the fashion,' she said as she spread the pictures before them.

Edith looked at the pictures and saw herself as a traveller preparing for a long journey, waiting for the sound of the violin so she might put her right foot forward.

'These gowns can be adapted to any design.'

Edith nodded and without so much as a glance pointed to the fashion plate nearest her.

'You don't care, do you?' said Flora.

Edith shrugged. No, she didn't care.

'The world is changing,' said Flora. 'Why should the village elders tell us what we can wear? I'll make you a most beautiful wedding gown.'

\*

The seamstress's sewing machine was reported to the village elders. The blacksmith's house and forge stood well away from the other houses in the village, which could only mean that whoever had heard it had gone out of their way to do so. That the seamstress was making a wedding dress for the cabinet maker's daughter was considered by the elders enough of an outrage to act upon. The girl must have bewitched the butcher for he would never have allowed it.

They went to the cabinet maker who was asleep. Edith had no intention of inviting them into the parlour as was the custom when dignitaries of the village paid a visit. Instead she ushered them into the kitchen. They stood together, these ancient ravens, these guardians of the old way of life that made progress almost impossible. If something hadn't been done before there was no need for it to be done now. The butcher, the most senior elder, was not among them.

'Where's your father?' a pencil-thin elder asked.

Edith didn't reply, neither did she offer them food or wine. The elders talked among themselves and then their spokesman, the miller, turned to her.

'You, girl, will be married in the traditional costume of this region and nothing else. Do you hear me?'

The six elders stared at her, awaiting an answer, and were struck by her beauty. None of them could remember her being this lovely for in the winter light she possessed an ethereal quality, a shimmer of snow-kissed skin. It was they who looked away first.

The cabinet maker appeared in the kitchen, unshaven, his clothes dishevelled. He was frightened to see the elders there.

'I'm going to stop,' he announced. 'The drinking. It's just that I've had a lot on my…'

The miller said, 'We're not here about that. We're here about the wedding dress.'

Edith's father was visibly relieved.

'We heard that the seamstress has been asked to make your daughter a wedding dress. We forbid it. Our ancestors laid down strict rules about dress for both men and women. This goes against all our beliefs.'

'It's not my doing,' said the cabinet maker, shuffling towards the table. He scraped back a chair and sat down.

'You must put an end to it,' said another elder. 'You

should never have indulged your daughter in this ridiculous notion in the first place.'

'I didn't. I never would,' mumbled her father again. He was eyeing the cupboard where the schnapps was kept.

'What did he say?' said one of the elders.

The thin man repeated the cabinet maker's answer.

'Then whose doing was it, if not yours?'

The question hung in the air, a ghost finding shape. The cabinet maker spoke his words clearly, so all could hear. 'The butcher's.'

'I don't believe you,' said the miller. 'The butcher is an upstanding member of this community, a man to be respected – he would never break with tradition.'

*

That Sunday the priest, being informed of what had happened, and fearing that his friend the butcher had been bewitched by the girl, took matters into his own hands with, of course, the Lord's blessing. In the pulpit he spoke of a well-known prophecy, unashamedly addressing Edith and the seamstress.

'When luxury and extravagance have spread so far over the face of the earth that everyone walks about in silken attire and when sin is no longer a shame, then the end of the world is not far off.'

His voice filled the rafters and though no one turned to look directly at Edith she felt all eyes upon her, particularly those of the butcher's two daughters.

'Few men will remain alive in this country, not more than can find a place in the shade of an ancient oak tree.'

Edith watched the faces of neighbours and friends as these words were spoken and it occurred to her that words were the weather by which they lived their lives; words that shaped their sense of self, stuck and stayed and grew them crooked or straight, loved or unloved. Words as changeable as the clouds that hung just as heavy on the living.

# CHAPTER ELEVEN

## FISH AND FABRIC

The butcher accompanied Edith home from church in silence. He never had been a man of many words. What he wanted to say that Sunday as they walked away under the watchful eyes of the congregation was just one word, a word that described an emotion that up to this moment he hadn't believed in. It belonged to a soppy-faced youth who trusted in happy endings. Love was not something a grown man indulged in. Yet this simple walk with Edith had for him a religious quality.

Edith's silence, her beauty, fascinated him. Her refusal to speak only made him want her more. Perhaps he hadn't loved her until she became silent. Her silence made her unapproachable. She reminded him of a painted Madonna. He would go down on bended knee before her and worship this ice virgin bride. And without meaning to he let out a laugh. For a thought had come to him: he had spent a lifetime saving every penny and now he was prepared to lay it all at her feet, a carpet of coins.

The priest had warned him. 'There can't be one rule for every other girl in the village and another for Edith. You're the head of the village elders and should know better. Has the girl bewitched you? I hope for both your sakes this isn't the case.'

What madness had possessed him to do such a foolish thing? Unless he put a stop to this nonsense he would have to step down from his position. He realised now that Edith had outwitted him. She had no intention of speaking up, she would wear whatever she was given without protest. It hadn't occurred to him that she would remain stubbornly silent for so long. What if she never spoke again?

The butcher could almost hear what his dead mother would have said. Edith had put a curse on him. He'd better take care for his mother had met the devil on her way to purgatory and he was waiting for her son at the crossroads, just as he had waited for her, to take them both to hell.

He pushed the thought from his mind. He and Edith would have a child. The idea thrilled him. Her flat belly would grow round, her small breasts would fill out. He would be the first and only man she had ever lain with. This time, he told himself, I will be patient. 'I will wait. I will change.'

It suddenly struck him that he had said the last sentence out loud. At her house Edith stopped at the gate and for the first time looked at him.

'For you I will be a better man than I was,' he said. Her expression didn't change. 'I know you don't love me but...' Each word a stepping stone across an emotional river.

Still her eyes didn't leave his face until, in the yard, she opened the door and he could tell she was not going to invite him in.

'I have to talk to your father,' he said by way of an excuse. 'He must pay the fine for not attending church.'

He followed Edith inside. Her father was half-dressed and drunk. The butcher, ignoring the cabinet maker, watched Edith. She walked past her father, hung up her shawl, took off her hat then let down the two white plaits that were wrapped round her head and undid them. She shook them out and her hair fell about her in a thick snowfall of white that she quickly twisted into a knot. The butcher was mesmerised.

'I know who has taken my daughter's voice,' said the cabinet maker suddenly. 'It's the bloodless.'

The butcher grabbed the blubbering drunk by the arm.

'Listen to me,' he said. 'Tomorrow you are to go and fetch the fish for the betrothal supper.'

'Fish?' repeated the cabinet maker, finding sobriety. 'How in this weather am I to get fish? We are all but cut off from the town.'

'Fish,' said the butcher, 'is the traditional food for a betrothal supper. I expect nothing less.'

And with that he left.

The cabinet maker waited until he was sure that the butcher's feet crunching in the snow were taking him away.

'And there I was worried about the bloodless,' he said. 'No, it will be a fish that puts me in my grave. If only you would speak up, Edith. A word from you would stop the wedding dress being made. Stop me having to risk my life for a fish. I've always done my best for you and yet you do and say nothing.'

Edith understood that she needed to keep her expression blank, that any sign of emotion would be fuel to her father's fire. When she had the power of speech there had always been rows. Arguing made him no better. He would shout and threaten, his sudden rages would drown out all she had to say. There are two people in a conversation, one person in an argument. Her father argued with the dead as if by shouting at the past he might bring back another chance, not just another bottle.

'Do you have no feelings for me?' he roared in her face. 'I built this house – with a staircase – for you and your grandmother.' At the word 'grandmother' he paused. 'It wasn't my fault what happened to her. I know you blame me. I did nothing. Do you believe me? Speak!' he yelled, his hand held high. 'How dare you not answer me. I am the head of this household.'

A king of small things, thought Edith as she backed away, knowing well the weight of her father's hand.

It was then that the door opened, letting in a sudden draught. The cabinet maker, fearing the butcher had returned, moved away from Edith.

'I didn't touch her,' he shouted at the unseen visitor.

Misha stood in the doorway. Edith took his hand and brought him into the kitchen. There was no doubting whose grandson he was. He looked like the butcher, but a kinder version of him.

'What do you want?' said the cabinet maker. 'Did your grandfather send you?'

'I'll come with you tomorrow and help you bring back the fish from the market. That's all.' He turned and left.

The cabinet maker followed him out into the yard. 'What time?' he called after the lad.

The following morning the air was freezing and the day had yet to find light. Edith was up. She had her father's snow boots waiting for him, fresh bread and cheese wrapped in a cloth. Yet she could not rouse him from his bed. Misha was already there with his grandfather's sleigh, waiting to begin the journey.

'Where's your father?' he said. 'We must start.'

Edith led him into her father's bedroom.

'Go away,' shouted the cabinet maker. 'Away. I'm not going to get out of my bed for a fish. I need my sleep. I'm not a well man.'

Misha shrugged. 'Leave him. It'll be faster if I go alone.'

Edith shook her head.

'It's all right,' Misha said and Edith handed him the food wrapped in the cloth, and one of her father's small bottles of plum brandy. 'Flora has asked me to collect a parcel from the draper's,' he added.

Edith wished she could say this betrothal is not worth the fish, not worth the fabric. Please don't go. But no sound came from her. After he had left, the house settled back into its silence.

I can't marry the butcher, she thought to herself. The inevitability of her fate sent a shiver through her. She would escape even if it was into the arms of death. She'd rather death danced her into the grave than let the butcher steal her youth, her life from her. She wondered if the walls of houses remembered conversations. If walls could speak they would tell the truth of what they recalled of the day she found her grandmother lying at the foot of the stairs.

# CHAPTER TWELVE

## BEYOND THE FOREST

Misha loved Edith, not as someone to marry, but as a sister and a friend. She alone of all the children he'd grown up with had never thought him an idiot. That was more than could be said for the rest of the community. Their perception of him as the village simpleton had not changed since he was small. Even his love of the mountain was taken as a sign of his mental inability rather than seen for what it was: his courage to make a pact with and survive in an inhospitable realm. The older he became the more he realised that it was his grandfather who was mostly responsible for this misunderstanding. He had terrified Misha since he was a child. At night Misha would still wake in a cold sweat, certain that the butcher was in his room.

Misha was five when he was caught taking an apple from the orchard, a crime that no other child in the village had ever been punished for. His grandfather had lifted him up as he would a squealing piglet, stripped the boy and taken his belt to Misha's tender skin. The beating had been of such severity that for a while no one was sure if the child would live. It was the only time he remembered his father being furious with his grandfather. He threatened to report him to the mayor. What surprised Misha even more was how angry his father had been with his mother.

The mayor's wife, Georgeta, had paid a visit to the invalid only when he was on the road to recovery. A tall woman, she said nothing and held a handkerchief to her nose. He had been lying on his front, unable to move. The room was hot and he had been impressed when with one flick of the handkerchief she had stunned a fly so that it fell to the floor, buzzing on its back. With a quick movement of her small boot she had squashed it. Then she bent down and gave him a book. As no one else had seen it happen, Misha hid it under his pillow.

'Very wise,' said the mayor's wife quietly.

It was from this book of fairy tales that Edith taught him to read; three years older than him, the little girl patiently spelled out the words as she had learned to do herself. Misha's mother never knew. Her conviction that he was an idiot was unbreakable. He had only the vaguest understanding of his mother's utter dislike of him. His father always excused her, saying that Misha had come too early and with his feet first. Misha, as children often do when there is nothing else to be done, accepted this irrational explanation as fact.

After the beating he felt that half his head was in the clouds. But worse than the beating was the bullying, the taunts of the other children who at the village school sang the word repeatedly. A leech of a word. Idiot. It sucked away all hope of anyone seeing him in a different light. The lack of love isolated him and because of his inability to hear he lived half in his head with his own thoughts for company, refusing to listen to the storm of words. Misha wondered at the God who had created this world and then put such an imperfect species on it as man.

Whenever he could, he would escape to the mountain, climbing through the birch forest to where the mighty pines stood tall and straight, guardians of the mountain range beyond. From sunrise to sunset he would wander without meeting another living soul. In the time he spent on the mountain he became accustomed to the daily companionship of eagles. Here, near the clouds, the air was so sweet – a heady wine – and he was free of the pettiness that whirled around his ferocious mother in the village below.

*

It had been late summer when he'd met the shepherd again.

'Do you remember me?' Misha had said when he'd come across him, high on the mountain one fine evening.

'Yes, Misha,' said Demetrius. 'It's good to see you again.'

He'd greeted him as if they were old friends.

'I've read the book you gave me – fourteen times.'

Demetrius laughed. 'Then you need another.'

Misha would not forget that night. They talked about

everything: about God, the mountain, and about Demetrius'
love for Edith. He said he counted himself richer than
any prince to have found her. When he played his violin,
Misha was entranced. How could such a heartbreaking
tune come from this instrument? The violin in the village
band grated even his poor hearing. Played well, it was the
music of the angels.

He asked Demetrius if there were words that went with
the melody. They were sitting round the dying fire, the moon
shining brightly, the sky still starry as the ghostly green light
of dawn crept across the horizon. Not a sound anywhere,
the flock quiet, the air alive with phantoms. The silence was
almost unbearable. Nature held its breath and the heartbeat of
the world stopped for an unimaginable second. The shepherd
whispered into the birth of a new day:

\*

*Full moon, high sea,*
*Great man thou shall be.*
*Redding dawn, cloudy sky,*
*Bloody death shalt thou die.*

\*

Before they parted Demetrius had given Misha a letter for
Edith. That day was the only day in Misha's life that he felt
that the word 'idiot' was his to wear.

The mist still clung to the mountain in ribbons and Misha, walking down the path, was taken aback to see a huntsman coming towards him. The young man was out of breath. He stopped and, mopping his forehead, asked Misha if he had seen a shepherd this way.

Misha didn't answer. He wasn't sure he'd heard him right for it seemed a strange request. He felt certain that Demetrius would have said if he'd been employed to help with a hunt.

'A shepherd,' the huntsman repeated, 'you fool.'

Misha shrugged and walked away. He heard and didn't hear the young man shout at him again. He went on, imagining how happy the letter would make Edith. The sun was bright, the mist had disappeared, the day was already hot.

The more he thought about the huntsman, the more Misha realised something was wrong. Where was the rest of the hunting party? The few huntsmen that came this way always hunted in twos or threes; some had dogs, some didn't, but they never hunted alone. He turned round and set off to follow the huntsman. Misha was fast on his feet and soon he saw the huntsman just above him, near where he and Demetrius had spent the evening.

Misha called out to him.

The sun was higher and blinding him. A shadow came in the shape of a giant.

'What are you doing up here?' said his grandfather.

'I've just seen a huntsman,' said Misha. 'I think he's lost.'

'He's not lost, he's with me,' said the butcher.

'But there's no good hunting up here,' said Misha.

Remembering the letter in his hand, he tried to slip it into his pocket.

'What have you got there?' said his grandfather. 'Give it to me.'

'No,' said Misha. 'It's not for you.'

His grandfather slowly took his gun off his shoulder and aimed it at Misha.

'I'd say it was a hunting accident. The sun was in my eyes and I thought it was…' He stopped. 'Give me the letter.'

Misha felt the blood drain from his face and lips, every bone in his body ready for flight.

The barrel of the gun hit him as he started to run. As he passed out he heard a single shot.

He had woken in the dark, blood in his mouth, his head whirling and a strange roaring in his ears. Instinct took hold and he crawled into a cave and slept. It was the sound of the rain that woke him, flooding his senses. He'd never heard the music of rain before, not like this, an orchestra of droplets of water falling on the rocks, dripping into the cave.

Misha went back to the village and never told anyone what had happened.

*

Like Edith, Misha had waited for the harvest supper and Demetrius' return. He would explain about the letter and by then it wouldn't matter. When Demetrius didn't appear, Misha felt sick to the pit of his stomach and implicated in the shepherd's disappearance in some way. Now it was too late and he couldn't explain what had happened even to himself, just as he couldn't explain why he could hear better than he had before being hit with the barrel of a gun.

The noise of words and the lack of quiet disturbed him. He found his own thoughts harder to hear and try as he might he couldn't remember the order of what had happened that morning on the mountain. Was it the huntsman or his grandfather he'd met first? The letter and the guilt he felt for those unread words sat as heavy as lead on his conscience.

The butcher had shown no surprise when his grandson had returned to the village, his face badly bruised.

'Accidents happen on mountains,' he'd said.

Since then Misha hadn't spoken to his grandfather and had done his best to avoid him. It had taken courage to ask if he might borrow his sleigh for the journey to town. He had stood a while at the butcher's door, his body twisted with nerves, his leg shaking beyond his control.

'What do you want?' The butcher filled the doorframe.

Misha backed away.

'The sleigh. I'm going with the cabinet maker to bring back the...'

He hadn't finished when his grandfather said, 'Come in.' Misha hesitated. 'Come in,' said the butcher again.

The house was untidy. Food from his breakfast was still on the table and a sea of things, half put away and half forgotten.

'This is why I need a wife,' said his grandfather as if

reading Misha's thoughts. 'Neither of my daughters think it fit or proper to come and help me. Why one has children…' He stopped, then said, 'The blacksmith…'

Misha's heart sank further. He would not discuss his employer with his grandfather. He braced himself for a cross-examination about the blacksmith's business. There was not much liking between the two men. Misha waited.

'He has a cuckoo clock.'

Misha had just seen it. 'A cuckoo clock?' he repeated. He waited for the word 'idiot'. It didn't come.

Instead the butcher said, 'I want one.'

Misha looked as stupid as he could without much difficulty, and said, 'Why?'

'For Edith. I want one for her. Not small, big. Bigger than the blacksmith's. Here.' And he gave Misha a bag of coins. 'I don't know how much such fandangled things are.' He stopped again. 'But fancy and in a box. Wrapped up. A gift.'

Misha took the bag and had reached the door when the butcher said, 'Misha.'

Misha slowly turned.

'Here,' said his grandfather. 'Take this for your trouble.'

Misha looked at the money he had been given and knew what he would buy. A gun.

# CHAPTER THIRTEEN

## THE WEATHER OF WORDS

Edith's grandmother believed that everyone was born with a secret number of heartbeats. Perhaps, thought Edith, it's the same with words. Once you had used them up, they were gone. All she could do now was listen. Even if she wanted to speak the only sound that would come from her would be an unbearable wail.

Grandmother had told her a story when she was a child. A long time ago, every man knew how many heartbeats he had in him, knew the hour of his death. So it was that God came to a village and saw a farmer mending a fence badly.

'That's sloppy work,' said God to the man.

The farmer shrugged. 'What's the point of building it well,' he said, 'when the fence will outlive me? In two days, I will be dead.'

God, being a tidy man, thought this was the wrong way to go about things, so he took away man's knowledge of heartbeats. Not knowing the day of his death improved things and man began to live his life with more purpose. It was a story that made Edith smile, the notion of God being tidy.

\*

Misha was expected back from the town in two days. On the morning of the first day, the butcher arrived at the cabinet maker's house unannounced. Edith couldn't think what he wanted, standing on the verandah with his hands stuffed into his pockets.

She showed him into the kitchen where her father sat at the table. He choked on a mouthful of bread when he saw the butcher.

'I want to talk to your father,' said the butcher. 'Alone.' He steered her out of the kitchen and closed the door behind her. She didn't move from the hall and the walls were thin enough to hear what was being said.

'She hasn't seen the doctor,' said the butcher. 'About her voice, I mean.'

'I can't afford the doctor,' said her father. 'Anyway, I thought you said you liked a silent woman.'

'There's something she must say if the betrothal is to go ahead.'

'That hadn't crossed my mind,' said the cabinet maker.

'Of course it hadn't,' said the butcher.

Edith thought that if the matter wasn't so serious it would be comical. She imagined Demetrius finding it so.

She answered a nervous knock on the front door. The doctor was a well-rounded man with a cushion of a face, his features almost lost in its puffiness. He followed her into the kitchen.

'Good,' said the butcher as the doctor took off his hat and coat and rolled up his sleeves.

'Sit here, Edith,' said the doctor. 'And open your mouth wide.' He held her tongue down with a metal spatula.

Edith stifled the urge to gag. She refused to give the men the satisfaction of seeing her body's utter revulsion at this invasion, at this pointless search for her words.

'Say "Aah".'

Silence.

Watched intently by the butcher and her father, the doctor felt her neck and took her pulse.

'Well?' demanded the butcher as if there might be something visible only to a doctor's eye that prevented Edith from speaking and might just as simply be cured. 'What's wrong with her?'

Edith could see the doctor carefully choosing his words.

'It may well be she has aphasia, a condition that…'

'I'm not interested,' said the butcher. 'Give her one of your tonics. And it better work.'

He strode out of the house, hitting the wall in frustration.

The doctor's cushion face was embroidered with beads of sweat. He rummaged in his bag and gave Edith a bottle of tonic.

'I sincerely hope you find your voice – for all our sakes,' he said as he left.

There is no medicine that could cure the pain that is frozen in me, thought Edith as she poured the tonic into the slop bucket.

*

It was on the evening of the second day that Lena came to visit Edith. She had been Edith's best friend since childhood. She came to her with a heart full of words that she longed for someone to hear; all of them a surprise.

Two years ago, autumn, the time of romance. The miller's son had come courting to the cabinet maker's house, his coin wrapped in ribbon, a token of his love. He asked Edith to be his bride and, being refused, went straight to Lena and on St Catherine's Day they had married. Lena's mother was a widow and both families were pleased with the match. Since then, there had been a distance between the two girls. Edith suspected that the miller's son, a dough-faced youth, hadn't hesitated to tell Lena that his first choice had been Edith. And now without a voice to ask if it was so, Edith had no way of knowing. She had hardly seen Lena since the harvest supper. Like many of Edith's friends, she stayed away, embarrassed by a silence they feared they might have contributed to.

'Is Misha back?' Lena asked.

Edith shook her head and wondered why her friend seemed so worried. Perhaps she too had asked Misha to bring something from the town.

'It will be dark soon,' Lena said. 'Do you think something's happened?' She came into the kitchen and stood by the stove. 'It's cold. I think this is going to be a brutal winter...'

Her words tumbled out of her, too fast. In all she had to say there was nothing of any interest. In an attempt to stop Lena talking, Edith put her finger to her lips.

'What is it? Do you hear his sleigh?' asked Lena, now agitated.

Edith shook her head and took her friend's hand. Lena, thrown by such kindness, began to weep.

'I have no one to tell,' she said.

Edith made tea and listened to the silence, to the gaps in the words, then she began to understand that Lena had come to her because her heart was broken.

'After I married, all my friends boasted of their pregnancies,' said Lena. 'Maria was having her second, and I wanted a baby so badly. I wanted a child more than I wanted a husband.' Lena twisted her handkerchief in her fingers. 'I used to think you could get pregnant from kissing. Stupid, I know. But no one told me. My mother said I would find out soon enough. You have to bear it and from it comes children. When we were first married, we kissed a lot, and nothing happened. Then Maria told me what she and her husband did to make babies. But when we tried it...' She stopped, put her handkerchief to her mouth.

'He couldn't...it would go limp. He said it was enough, and it was unpleasant. He would get out of bed and wash. I didn't know what to do. I thought there must be something wrong with me. My mother kept saying to me, "Lena, when will you do your duty and give me a grandchild?" Then my husband began to go more and more to the town, he would never say why, except it was to do with his father's business. When he told me he would be gone for a week, I asked if I could go with him. He said no. I asked why not, and he grew angry, said my duty was to have a baby and look after the house. Nothing more.

'When he left, I thought, this is my life, and I will never have a child. I will just have this dull man. He had been gone for three days. I'd had no visitors – our house, as you know, is out of the village. I felt so alone. Then one evening, as the sun was setting, I saw him, Misha, all golden, and an idea came to me. I thought even if he spoke about it, no one would believe him – after all, he is the village idiot. I took him up the stairs, I told him what he had to do. I lay down on the bed, pulled up my skirts. I lay still just like my husband said I had to and I didn't move.

'Misha laughed. He said, "No one can make a baby that way, not one that is full of life." I told him my husband said it was unpleasant to see me… down below. He said, far from it, and undressed me then kissed every part of me until I didn't know what to do and I let out a cry. I couldn't help it, never had I felt such pleasure. Then he did it all again and more. Four nights and four days, we made love, and it was love in its purest form… There now, tell me I will burn in hell for my sins.'

Edith put her arms around Lena and rocked her.

'Everyone thinks Misha is an idiot. Even his family. He isn't, he's intelligent. He told me, "If you do have a child, may he not be like me." I told him he was a kind, loving man. I hardly see him now, since the harvest supper when your shepherd didn't come. I know like my husband, Misha loves you, not me. It doesn't matter. Winter has come too soon. And all I do is think about the nights we spent together, and I yearn for him.

'I'm pregnant. My husband thinks it's his, that his fumblings are enough, that what he does is enough. He said that now it has happened we don't have to do it again, and we can live better lives without it. I thought I just wanted a baby and I do want the baby. But more or all of it is I want to be with Misha. I haven't yet told him about the child.' She blew her nose.

Edith cooked a meal for them both. After they had eaten, Lena stood up and said, 'I feel better. Some things are too heavy to bear alone.'

She was getting ready to leave when they heard the gate open.

'Misha's back,' said Lena, her cheeks flushed, and she ran to the door only to see her husband and Edith's father, arm in arm, zig-zagging across the yard.

'Time to go home, Lena,' said her husband. 'A lady with a baby needs to rest.' He laughed. 'See?' he said to Edith. 'See what you could have had?'

He leaned heavily on Lena as she walked him home.

*

Like heartbeats, Edith thought, we cannot know how many words there are in us. What she knew was that in stillness, she heard every word said to her in a way she hadn't before. There was an art to listening. She, unlike the priest, had no god to judge people by. Her gift lay in the power to hear and hold safe all that was said to her. She supposed that her silence was similar to the strongbox she'd seen in the mayor's office. A place for a woman to leave her secrets, confident that what was said to Edith would not be repeated.

*

'I'm going to bed,' said the cabinet maker. Only as an afterthought, he asked, 'Has Misha come back?'

# CHAPTER FOURTEEN

## A ROOMFUL OF HENS

Edith was up early the following morning. There still was no news of Misha. The day was bone cold, snow fluttered in an icy wind as she wrapped her shawl about her.

'Please may Misha be safe,' she prayed, though she didn't know who to.

It wasn't the god that lived in the village church, he was too mean to warrant prayers. It wasn't to the wooden Madonna. Who then?

She saw her grandmother. Yes, perhaps it's you, she thought as she opened the door to Grandmother's old room. There was hardly anything in it now; a bedframe, a chest and, perched on the beams, the hens that Edith had brought in last night. She gathered up the eggs and shooed them out into the yard. She was in the henhouse when she heard the latch on the gate. Hoping it might be Misha, she went to see but there were the butcher's two daughters.

She'd never liked them. As a child they had frightened her,

especially Vanda, the taller sister, Misha's mother. Whenever Edith had gone to Misha's house in the summer, there had been jars on the windowsill with a spoonful of jam in the bottom to attract the wasps. Lena said Vanda was a witch and she ate the wasps and that's where she got the sting in her tail.

Una was the smaller, rounder sister. She knew everything about everyone else's business and little about herself. Her daughter Sorina looked nothing like her; she was taller and striking in her appearance. It was, thought Edith, the most ridiculous notion that she would be a stepmother to these two crows. The idea made her feel sick. She watched them looking around the yard, eyeing up the house.

'A cabinet maker,' said Una. 'He should be ashamed of himself. Look at the state of this verandah – and the girl hasn't even swept the snow off it.'

'Lazy like her father,' said Vanda. 'What did I tell you?'

Edith had been dreading their arrival. It was a tradition that every bride should be tested by her mother-in-law or other family members to see if her housework was fair or indifferent.

What does it matter, she told herself. You have nothing to prove. Neither of them wants this any more than you. Perhaps if she failed this test, they might persuade their father not to go through with the marriage. She took a deep breath and went to meet them.

'There you are,' said Una. 'I could have slipped on these steps. Why aren't they swept? Answer me.'

Edith was growing into her silence. There was nothing she could say even if she wanted to. The sisters knew that, as did the whole village. Uninvited, they walked up the steps, helping each other into the house. They hesitated on the threshold. She could see they were impressed for Edith had an eye for making even a fallen-down house feel homely.

'Did you do the decorating yourself?' asked Una.

The main room had been painted with small scenes from the mountain and the village life. Edith nodded.

The two women reminded her of figures from a child's Noah's Ark, their wooden noses poking into cupboards and chests. Una's nose turned up, Vanda's turned down.

Edith went about her tasks, ignoring them as much as possible.

'What's that smell?' said Vanda, as she opened the door to Grandmother's room. A hen waddled into the kitchen and Vanda shooed it into the yard. 'You'll have to run our father's house better than this. Hens in a bedroom? That will never do.'

The sight of these two women, two spiders spinning a web from which Edith could not escape, made the wedding feel inevitable.

They talked. Oh how these sisters talked. They sounded to Edith as her hens did in the morning, full of pecking complaints.

'Girl,' shouted Vanda. 'Girl, did you hear me or are you deaf like my idiot son?'

There was no excuse for her silence, Una said. It was time

she spoke. The sisters agreed that no woman could remain silent so long; it was against her very nature. Not talking was an impossibility.

Una took hold of the broom and made a movement to startle Edith. Edith laughed.

'There. You see, she can laugh. Therefore, she can talk.' Edith stood her ground as Una made another lunge at her. 'A proper hiding,' said Una. 'That's what she needs. That's what she'll get when she's married our father, and no mistake. A proper hiding.'

The problem facing the sisters, Edith could see all too well, was that this slip of a girl would soon be their stepmother. What could they do?

'Goodness knows why our father should decide to marry again,' said Una. 'And why choose her?'

'No,' said Vanda. 'Did you see the way she kneads the dough?'

'And did you see the embroidery in her hope box?' said Una. 'With needlework like that she needs hope.'

They both laughed.

'Sister, that's funny,' said Vanda.

'I can only think she's bewitched our father,' said Una.

They leaned together, these two inseparable sisters.

'What if she never speaks again?' said Una.

'Leave her. It's no use. And why should it concern us?' said Vanda.

'It does,' said Una. 'What if she has a son?'

'Her hips are too narrow,' said Vanda. 'And anyway,

she might well collapse altogether under the weight of our father.' The sisters laughed. 'He'll make mincemeat of you, my girl.'

And the morning dragged on, longer than many mornings before. Edith spent the time wondering how she could escape the marriage. Her father, like most of their neighbours, found himself indebted to the butcher. Before she was born, her grandfather had had a thriving business and a wastrel of a son. In less time than it took to raise a child they had become the most impoverished family in the village, not even owning a horse or a sleigh.

She would need a sleigh to escape and whoever she borrowed it from would be in trouble with the butcher. She couldn't do that. It would have to be on her own without any help.

By midday, the sisters agreed there was not much to be done without the fish.

'We will be here tomorrow,' said Una. 'Early to start cooking for the betrothal supper. And I want to see this house tidy.'

'Tomorrow,' they said together, picking up their baskets.

*

It was late afternoon when Lena came again into the yard to ask, 'Has Misha come back? I don't know what I'd do if…' She stopped. 'Oh, Edith—' She took her friend's hand and kissed it. 'This is how you feel – I'm so sorry.'

No one knows how I feel, thought Edith. Everyone's loss is different. Misha will be back. She took Lena inside, made tea and they waited.

'I'll have to go soon,' said Lena, her eyes filled with tears. 'The miller's son expects his tea to be on the table on time.'

The women looked up as they heard the latch on the gate and footsteps on the verandah.

'Your father?' said Lena.

Edith shook her head. She knew too well the sound of her father's swaying steps. She went to the door where Misha was smiling, holding a fish wrapped in a cloth. Before he could say what had delayed him, Lena ran to him. Misha was surprised that she should have been concerned.

'I stayed at a farm. I thought it best to travel in daylight.' He stopped, seeing the tears in Lena's eyes. 'Were you worried about me?' he asked.

'I'm pregnant,' said Lena.

'You are?'

She nodded.

'That's good,' he said. 'It's what you wanted.'

He looked at Edith and realised that she understood the implication of what Lena was saying. Of course she did. Lena would have told her.

Lena moved away from Misha as they heard the sound of the gate. They waited, hardly daring to breathe, as if just by being seen together, it would be enough for their secret to be known.

The snow muffled the cabinet maker's footsteps. They

heard him cursing and then silence. Edith opened the door
and saw her father flat on his back in the snow. Misha helped
Edith get him to his feet.

'Have you got the fish?' asked the cabinet maker.
Misha gestured at the cloth parcel on the table. 'He's got the
fish, bring the man a drink! I tell you, Misha, the sooner this
bitch is off my hands, the better.' He went to the cupboard.

'Look at me, Edith. I'm taking another bottle of wine.
Because it doesn't matter. The more I drink, the more your
bridegroom brings me. You and your silence can go to hell.'
He wheeled round the room. 'Oh, here's little Lena,' he said
as she moved out of his way. 'Now, she's a sensible girl, she
got married.'

Misha said, 'That's as good as saying the vixen was
sensible to be caught in a trap.'

'Is that a joke?'

'No,' said Misha.

The cabinet maker sat down at the table. 'Sit, young man,
sit and have a drink with me.' He poured the wine into an
invisible glass. It ran onto the table and through the cracks.
Edith mopped it up.

'I think I've pissed myself,' her father said, laughing. He
stood, his trousers wet, and an acrid smell of wine and urine
filled the room.

Misha helped him to bed.

'I have to go,' said Lena when Misha returned.

Edith watched him walk Lena to the gate.

'Thank you for your silence,' he said as he came back

into the kitchen. 'You heard what I thought would never find a voice. One day, Edith, things will be better.'

She put her head to one side and with her arm played an imaginary violin.

'I will find him,' Misha said. 'I made a silent promise to you that I would. Did you hear it?'

Edith nodded. And realised she couldn't leave the village until she knew what had happened to Demetrius.

# CHAPTER FIFTEEN

## BETWEEN HER WORDS

Good as their word, Vanda and Una arrived early to help prepare for the betrothal supper. Edith heard them in the yard arguing about Una's daughter, Sorina.

'You made her go there on her own to clean our father's house?' said Vanda.

'Sister, I'm too busy to do it,' said Una. 'And it will teach her not to go talking rubbish.'

'She came to me, no one else, me, and told me what happened at the inn. You should take better care of your daughter.'

'Well, that's rich, coming from someone who has so little love for their own son. Don't tell me how to bring up my daughter.'

Edith opened the door and went out onto the verandah.

'You still haven't swept the snow from the steps,' said Una and, without so much as a good morning, bristled uninvited into the house and put her basket on the kitchen table. 'Is the parlour aired?' Receiving no reply, she snapped, 'I'm not going through another day of your childish silence. You'd better find your tongue or how can the rings be exchanged?'

'Enough,' said Vanda. 'Enough.'

'What?' said Una.

'You heard me.'

'What's got into you?' She sniffed. 'I see that Misha's back. I told you there was no need to worry. And still you bite off my head over nothing.'

Vanda patted down her skirt. 'Let's just get on with this.'

'There's certainly plenty to do. And this mute, stubborn girl to deal with. Is the dough rising? No. Is the table laid? No.'

'Quiet,' said Vanda. 'Leave it be. I've brought the bread. And cakes and biscuits.'

'Why didn't you tell me before we set off? Anyway, that isn't the point. The betrothal supper is a test to see how Edith is going to run our father's house. I would have thought…'

'Would you want to run our father's house and live under his roof again?' asked Vanda. Una didn't reply. 'As Edith has no voice I will say it for her: neither you nor I want to go near that pigsty.'

An awkward silence fell between the two sisters. Una went into the parlour and came back with the log basket.

'Here,' she said to Edith. 'Logs. Go and fill it now, girl.'

Edith didn't move. She didn't care if this meal was never cooked. If nothing was done she would consider it to be too much.

'Logs,' repeated Una.

To Edith's surprise Vanda said, 'Leave her.'

'Are you quite well, sister?' said Una. 'What's come over you? Why are you angry with me? Surely it's…'

'I'm angry at what we put up with,' said Vanda.

'What do you mean?'

'This. This betrothal.'

'I agree. Our father shouldn't be marrying again, especially not to…'

'That's not what I mean, and you know it,' said Vanda. 'What choice does Edith have? None. The elders, our father, the priest, all want this match. That shit, the cabinet maker, wants this wedding because our father will pay all his debts. Our father wants it because… because…'

'Sister,' said Una, 'this is terrible talk.'

'Is it? And what about Sorina?'

'What about her?' said Una.

'You turned your back, looked away, did nothing to protect her. She's just a child, Una, a child.'

'What are you talking about?'

'The hunting party – the young men that came up from town. Sorina told me what happened and you don't…'

'Oh, that,' interrupted Una, laughing. 'That was months ago. As I said, a young girl and her imaginings. It was nothing more than harmless fun.'

Edith wondered what had happened since yesterday to make Vanda more sympathetic to her. It must have been something serious but Una refused to hear what her sister was telling her in the space between her words. Edith thought about Sorina. It was true she was no longer a silly, fun-loving girl. She didn't laugh so much, she looked… defeated.

'Well,' said Una, 'I'll have to do it myself.'

'Yes, scuttle away,' Vanda called after her. 'Harmless fun.'

There was no reply. Vanda put a pile of potatoes on the table and started to peel them. They sat in silence, Vanda tutting under her breath.

Una came back with the logs, a martyred expression on her face. 'I've had enough of this nonsense. I told you, nothing happened to Sorina.' Vanda let one peeled potato plop into the pan. 'And quite why Sorina is telling you such tall stories, I don't know.'

'You don't know?' Vanda laughed. 'You must be the monkey that sees no evil. My son can hear none and Edith can speak none.'

'No harm done, maybe a little more wine was drunk than should have been.' Una laughed a forced laugh. 'Men will be men.'

'You foolish woman,' said Vanda. 'Do you really not know?'

The question hung unanswered and just then, to Una's relief, Flora arrived with Lena. Edith saw from the looks on their faces that they must have heard what Vanda had said.

Una put on her Sunday good deeds smile, determined now to be gracious. Edith made coffee. The cabinet maker emerged unshaven and half-dressed into a kitchen of women. He turned and went back into his bedroom. No one said a word.

The seamstress took the toile for the wedding gown from

her basket and hung it on the doorframe, a ghost of white calico. It spoke of a future that didn't belong to the traditions of the village or these women's lives.

'It isn't proper,' said Una. 'It's indecent. There's hardly anything of it. She will freeze.'

'It's going to be made in velvet,' said Flora.

'Such a dress as this can – and I am sure will – bring a curse on the wearer,' said Una. Then, as if she needed to be told again, she said, 'Whose idea was it in the first place?'

'Your father's,' said Flora. She put the tape measure round her neck. 'He usually gets what he wants, doesn't he?'

Edith went into the bedroom to undress and stood in her camisole while Flora transformed her into a creature of unearthly beauty. The women stopped what they were doing and moved close to each other to look at Edith. She was slight, almost fragile. They watched, mesmerised, while Flora pinned and tucked the calico, altering the shape to fit.

'Is this what grand ladies in town wear?' asked Lena.

'Yes,' said Flora. 'And even not so grand ones.'

'Do they have curses on their heads?' asked Vanda, looking at her sister.

'Not that I'm aware of,' said Flora.

A silence fell over the group and Edith could almost hear their thoughts.

*If I lived in the town that's what I would wear.*

*What would my daughter look like if she wore such dresses?*

*This will be the end of our world.*

*

By late afternoon the parlour had been made ready and the candles lit. Edith went into her bedroom, closed the door and opened her hope box. Every girl in the village had one. When she was five, her father had made hers and her grandmother had painted it with figures from a circus. She remembered them arguing over it, her father insisting it should have been painted in a traditional pattern not decorated with a load of vagabonds.

'Who are they?' Edith had asked.

'Clowns and acrobats from Zamfir's Circus.'

'What's a circus?'

Her grandmother had told her about the summers before Edith was born when she would travel with the circus, telling her stories.

To Edith, the hope box was magical. She dreamed of this mythical world and was sad to find the box was only for her wedding trousseau.

Now she took out the petticoats, the hand-embroidered skirt, the blouse and the bodice that she would wear for the betrothal supper. Once, when there was hope in her stitches, she thought she would marry a man she loved. Now she dressed knowing it was for nothing. Only the painted circus figures held a memory of when the world was full of possibilities, a hopeful place.

Lena knocked on the bedroom door and asked if she could help.

Edith's hair was tumbled down her back and Lena said, 'You always had such beautiful hair. I remember, I was so envious – no, I still am envious – of how thick it is. Your grandmother would call it Rapunzel's hair. I want to thank you for listening. I hope tonight that there might be a chance for me to talk to Misha.' She wound the two plaits round Edith's head and threaded evergreen and winter roses through them. 'There. You look beautiful.'

'Where's my wife?'

Lena jumped when she heard her husband's voice. 'I have to go – the guests have started to arrive.'

Edith closed her eyes.

*Be with me, my love. Stay close beside me for this should have been our betrothal supper.*

*Look for him to the right,*
*Look for him to the left.*
*Look for him straight ahead,*
*Look for him in the air.*
*And bring my shepherd back to me.*

When she opened her eyes she saw him in the middle of the room, holding his violin with its strings of light. He wore a hat with an eye at its centre. Demetrius smiled at her and one by one the strings of light disappeared into her.

*Even if I've imagined you, it's enough to give me strength. In your face I see my home.*

And the ghost of the shepherd vanished.

# CHAPTER SIXTEEN

## LET THE DEVIL TAKE
## THE CONSEQUENCES

'What is it, Grandpa?' Sorina asked when the butcher gave Edith his betrothal present.

The word 'Grandpa' visibly jarred the butcher. Vanda found the scissors.

'Here,' she said to Edith.

Edith took them and, in no hurry, cut the string and undid the wrapping paper.

Before Edith had taken her present out of the box, the butcher, unable to contain his excitement, said, 'It's a cuckoo clock,' and held it up for the assembled guests to see.

There followed much talk as to where such a handsome clock should be hung.

'Of course,' said the doctor, 'it will only be here for a short while as Edith will soon be taking it to her bridegroom's house.' The butcher smiled. The doctor, only half laughing, added, 'I can't make up my mind who is the most fortunate

– the bridegroom for having such a beautiful bride or the bride for having such a generous husband.'

This is what the butcher has worked for, thought Edith. She saw his fingertips dipped in the blood of slaughtered animals, dipped in the blood of her shepherd. She had no proof that the butcher was his murderer; she had no doubt of his guilt. She saw the workings of his mind as simpler than the cuckoo clock's. What if she was wrong, she wondered, and her love wasn't dead? She looked up with such hope when the door opened, letting in the snow.

'Sorry we're late,' said the mayor, stamping the snow off his boots and taking a basket from his wife. He handed it to Edith. 'A small offering,' he said.

Georgeta stood beside her sickly son, the university student, an earnest young man who had probably looked forty when he was four. Their arrival caused a flurry among the guests and annoyed the butcher. He wanted no one upstaging him at this important moment when a decision had to be reached.

'There,' said the butcher, pointing.

And the cabinet maker, with one unsteady blow of his hammer, drove the nail into the wall. A thin stream of plaster fell to the floor. The cuckoo clock was placed just above where the bride and bridegroom would sit. The butcher had already set the clock at his house the night before to make sure it worked. He turned to the guests.

'On the hour,' he said, 'the cuckoo comes out from here—' he pointed to a small door at the top of the clock, 'flaps its wings, opens its beak and speaks. Then a dancing couple go round and round and a man chops wood.'

There were gasps of wonder that such a thing was possible.

'Aren't you lucky,' said the mayor, 'to have such a thoughtful husband?'

It surprised Edith that people waited for her to speak, as if the notion of not speaking was an affectation that could be put away when the occasion demanded. Such as now when rings were to be exchanged.

The priest, a man who looked as if he could pass unseen through the cracks in a wall, puffed himself up.

'Before we sit down to dine on what I'm certain will be an excellent meal,' he said, to a low mumbling from the guests, 'there is the important matter of the exchange of rings. I call forth the bridegroom.' The butcher stepped forward. 'I call forth the bride.'

The cabinet maker came up behind Edith and pushed her towards her bridegroom. The butcher was wearing an embroidered coat that had fastened when he was a younger man but now gaped over his belly. The sight of what appeared to be a grizzly old bear taking a faun to be his wife made the company uneasy. The priest took the rings from the cushion on which they'd been placed and blessed them.

'Do you take this woman to be your wife?'

The butcher, impatient for it to be over, took hold of the ring. 'I do,' he said.

'Do you, Edith, take this man to be your husband?'

Only the ticking of the clock could be heard.

'Edith,' said the priest, 'do you take this man to be your husband?'

The room held its breath.

'Cuckoo cuckoo,' answered the clock.

The little bird flapped its wings, the dancing couple went round and round, the woodcutter chopped wood and the butcher stared at the priest.

How many men, thought Edith, are in the pocket of my husband-to-be?

'I take that to be "Yes",' said the priest and the guests clapped, eager for their supper.

'But she didn't say anything,' said Sorina.

'Quiet,' said her mother.

The butcher put the ring firmly on Edith's finger. It was too loose. The one she put on his finger was too small. Make of that what you will, she thought.

'They will be altered before the wedding ceremony,' said the butcher. Then, spreading his arms wide, he invited them all to the wedding in two weeks' time.

Edith sat next to the butcher. The butcher demanded more wine.

'Why are you women so slow?' he said.

The men laughed, the women didn't. The fish was brought in.

I can't do this, thought Edith. I will not do this.

As the meal progressed the butcher manoeuvred himself closer to the priest and the mayor to talk business and to make sure that everyone knew he was the head of the elders and that not even a wedding dress was going to make him relinquish the position.

Edith had seen the relief on the faces of both the butcher and her father when the rings had been exchanged. At least this part of the contract had been upheld. Sitting alone she felt an unbearable sadness at what might have been. If it were Demetrius seated next to her this would have been the happiest moment of her life. She felt herself to be inside her coffin in the vestibule of the church, the congregation milling round her, waiting for the lid to be nailed down. For a moment the room spun.

After supper a small band of musicians – not one of whom had an ear for music – started to play and the tables were pushed aside for dancing. No one could quite put a finger on when or why it had begun but an undeniable sadness mingled with regret hung over the party and as soon as it was considered polite the guests began to leave. Before Flora left she asked if she could bring the dress in the morning for a fitting.

The cabinet maker was asleep in a chair and Edith saw no point in waking him.

'You liked your present?' said the butcher. She never took her eyes off him and under such a bright glare he felt ill at ease. He brushed the thoughts from his mind. 'I think it was a great success.'

He moved to kiss her and Edith stepped away.

'We have enough time,' he said and picked up his hat.

*

When the last guests had left, Edith took down the cuckoo clock, pulled the cuckoo free from its cage and affixed her ring to it. She found a small box, and placed the cuckoo and the ring inside. Her father raised his head to see his daughter at the door in her coat.

'Going to the butcher's house?' he asked. 'Good... good...' and he fell asleep again.

Taking a lantern she set off, the snow whirling about her.

In the darkness of her thoughts, she said, '*Oh my love, walk beside me.*'

'*I'm beside you still.*'

At the butcher's house she knocked on the back door. The butcher, who had taken off his coat and unbuttoned his trousers so he might breathe more easily, was shocked and excited to see Edith standing there.

'Come in,' he said.

Edith shook her head and handed him the little box. He made a move to take hold of her but Edith was faster and before he had opened the door wide she was gone. He had to admit he was too drunk to go after her. Anyway, he told himself as a mouse scuttled across the floor, best she doesn't see the house in this state.

He took the box into the kitchen and cleared a space on the table with the back of his hand. He poured himself a plum brandy, wondering if it was a piece of embroidery she had given him as a thank you for the clock. He opened the box. The ring and the broken cuckoo lay there, a metal hairpin stabbed through them. He gasped for air. Only then did he realise what a fool he was, that this marriage was an old man's fantasy. He looked up to see the ghost of his mother sitting at the table.

'She will never love you,' said the ghost of his mother.

'Go away and leave me be,' said the butcher.

'You know what you want to do,' said the ghost. 'What you would love to do. It would be so easy.' She put her long fingers to her neck. 'Just press here.'

'Mother, go,' said the butcher.

A graveyard grin crossed her features. 'All I am saying, son, is you'd better make sure she doesn't run away before the wedding or you will never have your little pleasure.'

His mother was right. She knew what it was he wanted, always understood the devil within him. He shuddered at the thought of the untold satisfaction it would give him to strangle the life out of Edith just after he'd taken her virginity.

'And the devil,' he said, throwing his glass across the room at the ghost, 'the devil can bear the weight of the consequences.'

# CHAPTER SEVENTEEN

## A DIFFERENT PAIR OF SHOES

Demetrius stood at the end of Edith's bed.

'*We can travel in these hours of sleep to the realm of otherness.*'

'*Then take me there.*'

In the yard the walnut tree was in blossom. Demetrius was beside her, which was strange as this had happened a long time ago when her grandmother was alive and she had been small. It was in this tree that she had first seen one of the bloodless, an old woman with a shawl wrapped round her head. Her hands were big, her nails long, her eyes black. In the midnight hour she used to call to Edith to come to her.

She sat in the branches now among the walnut blossom, saying the same words as she had before, words that frightened the child in Edith because she hadn't understood them.

The woman told her that her son had sold her to the filth man. The filth man had terrible breath and rotten teeth and talked about his dead dog. The filth man made her sleep in a coffin with a stone on her chest. She was waiting to take her son to hell.

'Someone must go with him for he can't take you,' she said.

As is the way with dreams that fail to connect, Edith found herself once more alone, waiting in the dark for the dawn. She wondered if there was a road that would lead her to that other realm, where she would be able to walk with Demetrius to another end, to a new beginning.

\*

'I'm sorry if I'm too early,' said Flora as she shook the snow from her skirt. 'It's truly treacherous out there. I can't remember a winter when it's snowed as much as this.'

Edith stoked the stove, put on the kettle to boil and waited for some warmth to return to the kitchen. As if she was a magician producing a rabbit from a hat, Flora took from her basket a creamy-white velvet dress. Edith couldn't imagine being dressed like that every day. How would you do anything other than stand still and eat nothing? Flora told her about her clients, these women who belonged to a different world.

'After this fitting,' she said, 'it's just a matter of adding the finishing touches. I had some of these left over from another design…' she showed Edith a box of shining white gems, 'I thought I'd sew them onto the bodice.'

Edith was transfixed by the dress that had so little to do with her.

There was no mirror in which Edith could see herself, only the reflection in the window and the look in Flora's eyes. Her body seemed different in the dress. It held her tighter, more upright, and she felt powerful. A dress like this was a suit of armour.

Flora had a mouth full of pins when they heard a loud knocking on the front door. Taking the pins from her mouth, she asked, 'Shall I see who it is?'

Edith shook her head. She knew it was the butcher come to shout at her or worse for having broken the cuckoo clock.

'Where's Edith?' He sounded angry.

They could hear the cabinet maker complaining, then what the men were saying was lost in a muffled conversation.

Edith braced herself. She stood tall as the bedroom door was thrown open.

'Why did you do that to the present I gave you? Do you know how...'

He stopped, his rage instantly evaporating as he stared at the vision before him. Edith was almost unrecognisable and even more desirable than when he'd last seen her.

Flora said, 'It's unlucky for the groom to see the bride in her wedding gown before the ceremony.'

Her words broke some spell for the butcher shook himself and without another word he left, ignoring the cabinet maker who went back to bed.

Flora closed Edith's bedroom door.

'What was that about?' said Flora, not expecting an answer. 'Now, put on your shoes and I'll fix the hem.'

The shoes belonged to Lena, but Edith wasn't able to find them. Her boots, she realised, were missing too.

'Never mind,' said Flora. She helped Edith to stand on a chest while she pinned the hem. She unlaced Edith who quickly changed back into her embroidered skirt, blouse and bodice. She sat on the bed as Flora folded everything away. When she'd finished she sat next to Edith.

'There's a reason that I wanted to come early this morning,' she whispered. 'We've been thinking, my brother and I. We've decided to help you escape from the village. So tomorrow my brother will be here before dawn. Look for his lantern. I have some money I can give you.' Edith shook her head. 'Is it because you want to marry the butcher?' Edith shook her head vigorously. 'Is it because you're worried that the butcher would take revenge on us?'

Edith nodded emphatically.

Flora took Edith's hands. 'My brother and I aren't staying in this village. Come the spring, we'll be gone. I think we can weather the storm with the butcher. We are probably the only people here who owe him nothing. So just be ready. Don't look so worried.'

She gazed at Edith for a moment then said, 'I too have kept silent. There's no one in this village I can tell except you — not because you have no voice but because you listen. Even when I'm saying far too much you hear me. It's a gift you have — to hold the words of others and to understand without judgement. Which is more than can be said for the priest.'

Edith gently squeezed her hand.

'It's about my brother, the blacksmith. I've loved him all my life and he me. There was no one else I ever wanted to be with. When our parents died we began to sleep together in the same bed and… and… I was very ashamed of what we'd done and we agreed it would never happen again. It was hard for both of us. Then one day we found a box of my father's papers and there it was: the man I thought was my brother was gypsy-born and had been sold to my father in exchange for three packets of tobacco.

'After that, we slept together and made sure no one in the village found out. In the spring I would go to work in the town and we began to save so that one day we might live there. A year ago, I found I was pregnant. We took the paper with us to a lawyer and asked if we could marry. He said that if the letter was authentic, he could see no reason why not.

'I gave birth to a little girl. We couldn't bring her home so we arranged that she would board at the Schmidts'. She's nine months old and we plan to move away from here in the spring, start afresh with our baby. I've told no one this but you. Don't stay. This village is a place of ghosts, it will suck the life from you. Tomorrow,' Flora whispered, 'you will be gone. Think of that.'

*

It was late afternoon and already the night was falling in on them when the cabinet maker emerged from his bed. Edith pointed at his boots then at her own homemade shoes and held up her hands, questioningly.

'How should I know?' said her father.

Edith felt like screaming. If she had a voice she would scream so loudly the windows would shatter and he would be putting his hands over his ears.

'Those shoes will do nicely,' he said, putting on his coat. She pulled at him and he turned on her and pushed her away. 'The butcher took them as a precaution. He doesn't want you running off. I want you married, and when you're married, he will buy you a new pair of boots.'

If I had the strength, thought Edith, I'd throw you out of this house. I would make you crawl on your hands and knees to the butcher and bring my boots back.

The cuckoo clock whirred into life. The dancing couple came out silently, the woodman chopped silently, but there was no cuckoo to mark the passing hour.

Concluding it was broken, the cabinet maker opened the little door and stuck his finger in. 'It's gone,' he said. 'The cuckoo's gone. It must've flown away.'

\*

Edith spent the evening trying to improve the homemade shoes. Then she burst into silent laughter and went into her grandmother's bedroom. For warmth, she'd brought the pig in as well as the hens. Edith opened Grandmother's chest and, under layers of clothes, embroidered tablecloths, nightgowns and blouses, she found what she was looking for: her grandmother's boots.

*

That night the snow fell heavy, the wind chasing it into every crack and cranny in the house. Edith waited in the dark for the dawn, for the light of a lantern. And knew before daybreak that the blacksmith wasn't coming. The blizzard made the journey impossible. She went to bed, curled into herself and wept. Nature had locked and bolted the door. There would be no escape for her.

She woke to find the world quiet, the light different; she got up and pulled back the shutters. The village lay buried in drifts of snow that brought with it an unearthly hush. It looked to Edith as if a new world was being fashioned, the old one buried.

*

'Edith!' Misha called from the verandah. 'I need your help.' He came into the kitchen. 'Should the pig be in here?'

Edith nodded.

'Listen, there isn't much time. The mountain is talking. It's cracking. I told the blacksmith and he too hears strange sounds. I think it's a sign there'll be an avalanche.'

Edith listened and didn't wait. She put on her grand-mother's boots, her coat and shawl and, with Misha's help, shoved the pig into her father's room.

'Only once, well before I was born, did such a catastrophe come near our village,' said Misha as they trudged through the deep snow, the wind blowing it one way then the other. 'The worst of it happened to the east. There were no houses there then but now the house of the miller's son is there. I went this morning to tell him it would be best if he and Lena left and went somewhere safer. He threw me out, told me I was an idiot. I don't know what to do. I thought if you went... I know you can't talk but...' He stopped. 'I'm worried about Lena.'

Edith set off towards the house of the miller's son and Misha was about to follow when she shook her head. He said something that she didn't catch in the whirling wind and after a few steps she looked back and Misha was gone.

The further she went, the more the houses disappeared into the snow. By the time she saw Lena's house, her black skirt was white and her feet and hands freezing. Now she could no longer hear the mountain, only the miller's son shouting. Edith banged on the front door and waited. The miller's son stopped shouting and she banged again and again until at last he opened it. Uninvited, Edith went into the house.

'What do you want?' said the miller's son. 'It's no one else's business what goes on between man and wife.'

Lena was holding her face, sobbing, but the moment she saw Edith she fetched her shawl.

'You can't leave in this weather, Lena,' said the miller's son, standing in front of the door. Edith stared at him, unblinking. He shouted, 'I have the right to punish my wife. A woman needs to know her place.'

And Edith's eyes never left his until he moved out of the way. Lena took Edith's arm as they set off.

The miller's son laughed. 'You won't get far. And I might not have a mind to open the door when you come back, freezing, begging to be let in.'

He slammed the door and turned the key in the lock. He can't keep out an avalanche, thought Edith.

Lena sobbed silently, her body shaking, her head bowed, but she matched Edith's determined steps. The sky was grey with snow and in all the whiteness everything looked the same. The path they had taken was unclear. Edith held tight to Lena's hand and knew that she hadn't enough clothes on for this weather. It was the baker's shop she saw first. The main street was deserted; no one would venture out in this weather. The snow in the cabinet maker's yard was up to the verandah. She opened the door and the warmth that greeted them possessed a presence, the ghost of her grandmother waiting to hold them in her warm embrace.

Edith found clothes for them both to change into. Lena not only had a black eye but bruises on her arms.

'Everything I do is wrong,' she said. 'And I think he knows he's not the baby's father.'

Edith shook her head; she doubted that the miller's son had the wit to work out that the child wasn't his. If he did, it was a truth so buried in him he wouldn't know what to make of it.

Lena was still shaking. 'The food isn't cooked to his liking and he always wants something I haven't made. His mother told me that I don't keep house the way I should and he said this morning he wants his mother there when the baby is born as I wouldn't know what to do for the best.'

Edith put her arms around Lena and gently held her. She looked so broken.

It was midday when the cabinet maker rose from his bed, seemingly oblivious to the pig.

'What happened to your eye?' he said, sitting down in front of a bowl of soup.

Edith didn't bring wine so he got up and fetched a bottle. He had just pulled the cork when the soup dishes started to move on the table.

'What's that?'

Edith knew. She opened the cupboard under the stairs and gestured to Lena and her father to go inside. They crouched there as Edith crawled in after them and closed the door.

'The mountain giant is awake,' said the cabinet maker.

'Why are we in here?' said Lena.

'It's the strongest part of the house,' said the cabinet maker.

They heard a roar as if the mountain had found its voice.

'It's started,' said the cabinet maker. 'It's the sleeping dragon. Or perhaps the devil's scholar who lives at the heart of the mountain. Or perhaps, daughter,' he put the bottle to his lips, 'perhaps it's your wedding dress that's the cause. I'm right, aren't I?'

The answer was furious. It vibrated through the house, rolled over the rooftops, shattering windows with a wave of snow and all the debris it had gathered in its path. Stones, trees, everything and anything came upon them with the speed of revenge. Then just as fast came the silence, a terrifying quiet.

As Misha had predicted, the avalanche had come from the eastern slope. A sea of snow thundered down the mountain with ferocious momentum, uprooting trees as if they were kindling, rocks stripping the side of the mountain of its thick winter coat. The sheer force and speed had exploded through the house of the miller's son, burying what remained in deep, churned snow, and still it rolled onwards in a wave of majestic fury down the mountain towards the town. The farms below that had taken a generation to establish were destroyed in an instant. Only the wide-eyed penned animals knew what was coming. As for Edith's village, the debris from the avalanche cascaded over the rooftops, shattered windows, and peppered the buildings with small rocks. It not only shook the earth, it shook everything and everybody, and nothing would feel safe again.

# CHAPTER EIGHTEEN

## THREE COFFINS

Lena's mother, hearing her daughter was alive, rushed to the cabinet maker's house, tears streaming down her cheeks.

'Oh, your face,' she said to Lena, seeing the marks. 'You've been injured.'

'Yes, Mother. This is what my husband did to me after Misha came to tell us to leave.'

'Why?' asked her mother.

'Because he didn't believe Misha when he said there would be an avalanche.'

'You can understand that,' said Lena's mother.

'What can you understand?' asked Lena. 'Misha coming to the house or my husband giving me a black eye?'

'There, there,' said her mother. 'It's shock, that's all.'

'No,' said Lena. 'Even if my husband is alive, I am not going back to live with him again. Never.'

She undid her blouse.

'What are you doing?' said her mother. 'Don't take your

blouse off.' Embarrassed, she looked to Edith for support. 'Thank you, Edith, for bringing...' She stopped when she saw the bruises on her daughter's arms and back. 'I'm sure he only did that because he cares for you.'

'Do you really believe that, Mother?' said Lena. 'He didn't care for me at all.'

'Calm yourself, Lena. Let me take you home.'

This is why so many of Grandmother's stories are about women escaping their mothers, lovers and princes, and transforming themselves into someone else, thought Edith. Without such stories what future would any girl have on this mountain? Lena had been lost. She had grown out of the story told her by her mother into a story she told herself.

'You never wished that I might be happy,' said Lena. 'All you wanted, all his mother wanted, all I thought I wanted was a baby.' She wiped her eyes. 'The miller's son couldn't even give me that.'

Edith put an arm around her and pointed to her bedroom, then to herself.

'You wouldn't mind?' Lena asked Edith.

Edith shook her head.

'Mind what?' asked Lena's mother.

'I'm staying here.'

Her mother was shocked. 'No you're not, you're coming home, you must. What would I tell the neighbours?'

Lena laughed. 'Tell them your daughter is having Misha's baby. Tell them I love him, not the miller's son.'

Words are like avalanches, thought Edith. Boulders of truth come crashing down on family stories until all is rubble.

The widow slapped Lena across the face. 'If what you say is true, there is a word for a girl like you. A word.'

'What I say is true. And there is a word for a husband like mine,' said Lena. 'A word.'

Her mother left, bright red with rage.

Lena started to shake. 'I've never spoken to her like that. I wouldn't have dared before today. She won't forgive me.'

She will, thought Edith.

Later the doctor called, sent by Lena's mother to make sure the baby was unharmed.

*

In the frantic days following the disaster, the community came together with spades and poles and dogs to find the bodies of the missing. Vanda was there, desperately searching for her son, her tears frozen on her face. At night she was the last to leave.

The mayor made enquiries in order to find out where the missing persons had been when the avalanche struck. The miller told him, shamefaced, that early on the morning of the avalanche, Misha had come to his house.

'Far too early – it was only just light. I mean, no one but a madman would be out in such a blizzard. He told me he'd been to my son's place to warn him.'

'To warn him of what?' asked the mayor.

'The avalanche. He said he'd told my son the snow was cracking and that he and Lena were in danger.' The miller admitted that, like his son, he'd sent Misha away, adding, 'After all, the boy's an idiot.'

His wife had agreed that Misha's warning was nonsense.

The miller repeated her last words as she left. 'I'm going to see if my son is safe. His useless wife won't know what to do.'

She never returned.

After a week of digging, two bodies were recovered from the wreckage of the house. The doctor said he thought that the miller's son and his mother hadn't suffered much, that it would have been a quick death. Misha remained missing and was thought to be dead. The search for him was called off. The villagers would have to wait until the spring for the snow to return his body. Only Vanda went on digging.

People said, 'That's what happens when you have a guilty conscience.'

'I know why you're silent,' Lena said to Edith. 'It's because there are no words to describe the grief you feel.' Lena took her hand. 'Misha's alive,' she whispered. 'He will be back.'

It seemed most unlikely to Edith. For what good reason would he disappear into the mountain during an avalanche?

Lena's mother came again to the cabinet maker's house, full of righteous indignation. She'd heard of the last words of the miller's wife.

'I've made your room ready and found your old cradle in the attic,' she said.

Lena said nothing but she went home with her mother.

What was said can't be unsaid, thought Edith, and Lena's mother would have had to dig a deep grave within her to bury the knowledge of who the father of her grandchild was. She would sow many small lies over the truth.

For once Edith's father had employment. Two bodies found, three coffins made. When they were ready, the blacksmith, who was also the village undertaker, made sure the bodies were washed, dressed in their finest clothes and laid out in the coffins that he then took on a sleigh to the church to await the funerals.

On Sunday the village gathered for the service. The open coffins lay side by side while the villagers said their farewells and when the lids were hammered down, the blacksmith took them back to the forge where they would stay in an outhouse until the snow melted and the earth was ready to receive them. One empty coffin remained with the cabinet maker, waiting for Misha's body to be discovered.

Lena didn't attend the funeral as the doctor had insisted she rest and keep as still as possible. He prescribed medicine that made her sleep. As for the cabinet maker, he might have been a drunken old fool, but Edith was in no doubt it was he who was responsible for seeding the idea in the fertile minds of a frightened community that the avalanche was caused by a white wedding dress. A simple notion, but one that appealed to the village elders. The butcher paid a visit to Flora to tell her she could stop work on the wedding dress as Edith wouldn't be wearing it.

The full magnitude of the disaster had to come home to the villagers. The only road to the town was barricaded by boulders and fallen trees. The debris of the avalanche created an impenetrable ice wall and there was no hope of anyone leaving the village until spring. The small community knew they were utterly cut off from the outside world. Once again, they were reminded of how precarious their lives were. The mountain giant still rumbled and the wedding hadn't been mentioned again.

The thought that the marriage might not happen occupied the sober part of her father's mind. Not out of concern for neighbours or for his daughter, but out of a terror that her worth as a bride might be lost to him and his debts would be left hanging around his neck. He had been twice to see the butcher and both times the butcher had refused to speak to him. The cabinet maker heard that Flora had been told the wedding dress was no longer needed. Even the butcher was talking of having been bewitched by Edith.

'What does it mean – bewitched?' asked the cabinet maker of anyone who would give him the time of day. 'Bewitched,' he said, over and over again.

And he worried – oh, how he worried – that Edith wasn't in the first flush of youth. She would soon be twenty-one and the butcher had been asking for her hand since she was sixteen. A cold dread came over him.

'What shall I do if he doesn't marry you?' he shouted at Edith. She could see him mentally adding up all he owed and the figures fermenting in his mind. 'We'll starve. We'll be ruined.'

The word 'ruined' interested Edith. That's what her future had been. That's what her life with her father was. That's what all her days would be if she was married to the butcher. And she thought that out of the ruin of her silence another language had been born. If there were no words to trip her up then her soul could travel faster. Perhaps it was the only way to find Demetrius.

Fear began to take hold of the villagers as the bleakness of their situation became more and more apparent. They would have to survive on what they had put aside. They were permanently cold and prayed that illness wouldn't strike. The elders asked the head of each household to be honest about what they had in the way of provisions. How much animal feed, how much fuel, how many candles – the list went on. The results would be announced that Sunday at church. All agreed that no one had bargained on such a hard winter or such a tragedy.

There was a need to find something or someone to blame. The wedding dress, they said, had a lot to answer for. It was agreed it had brought bad luck.

Superstition held the village together, that and fear of the unknown, be it the Lord or the devil, the traveller or the stranger. Or even a wedding dress. Fear was the invisible fence, sunk into the earth by tradition.

# CHAPTER NINETEEN

## PIG'S BLOOD

The butcher wouldn't hear of his wedding being postponed. He had argued with the elders that the village needed something to celebrate – even if his grandson's body hadn't been found. It made little difference if Misha was buried or not for there could be no doubt that the lad was dead.

'The wedding will bring the village together,' said the butcher, 'give people hope in these dark days. There'll be a feast to look forward to.'

Here the other elders felt themselves to be on safer ground. The butcher couldn't possibly expect neighbours to dig deep into their stores now they were cut off from the rest of the world. Every morsel of food was vital to their survival. What would happen if the winter weather worsened and lasted longer than usual?

The butcher made light of their complaints.

'What?' he said. 'An egg, a spoonful of flour, a cup of cream? That won't leave anyone starving. And tradition is tradition.'

To which the elders had no argument. He had, after all, accepted their counsel and abandoned the foolish notion of his bride's wedding dress.

'You're right to be cautious,' said the butcher gravely. 'And thinking of how we'll all survive this winter, I might need my loans repaid.'

He took out the small, leather-bound notebook in which the sums owed to him were written, and turned to the miller. 'Shall I start with you?'

'No need,' said the elders as one. 'The wedding will take place as planned.'

The butcher put away his notebook.

*

That Sunday when the congregation was told of the wedding arrangements, a murmur of disbelief went round the church until the priest called them to prayer. Only Edith didn't kneel. She remained standing, watching the priest, knowing the words he spoke were corrupted by the butcher's orders. He peddled guilt in order to soften his flock to relinquish their food supplies. If she had a voice, she would have screamed: save your food – don't waste it on this wedding.

Making no effort to be quiet she walked out of the church, allowing the large wooden door to slam behind her. Her act of rebellion was noted by everyone.

Una was kneeling next to her father. His elbow jabbed her ribs.

'Bring her back,' he hissed.

Once outside, she called after Edith. 'Come back this minute. Where do you think you're going?'

Edith ignored her. She heard Una run up behind her and felt her shawl being pulled from her shoulders. Only then did she turn to face her.

Una stamped her foot. 'How dare you walk out of church like that? Do you think you're above us all? I know this holy silence of yours is a sham. I see through you, you little bitch.'

Edith remained expressionless and started to walk away. Una caught her skirt.

'Don't you dare turn your back on me!'

Losing her temper to righteous indignation Una attacked Edith, her small hands aiming to slap Edith's face and missing. Edith didn't flinch nor take her eyes off hers until Una ran out of steam and became conscious that she looked an ass. Defeated, she returned breathless to the church.

Since the avalanche, Edith hadn't heard Demetrius in her head or seen him in her dreams. Don't give up now, she told herself, you will find him again.

Vanda hadn't been in church and the news that her father had no intention of postponing the wedding was almost enough to send her mad. Later that morning she went to see him. Heart pounding, her legs shaking, even the sight of him filled her with revulsion. She found him slitting open pigs, pulling out their insides into a bucket.

'This wedding must wait until the spring,' she said. 'It isn't right to hold it now, not with Misha gone.'

'Isn't it what you wanted?' her father said without looking up at her.

'What do you mean?'

'To be free of that idiot.'

In a blind fury, she ran at him, knocking over the bucket. He put his hand on her face and shoved her away. Vanda fell backwards and he stood over her, his knife in his hand.

'Why didn't you come to clean my house?' he said, kicking her sharply. 'Why send Sorina?'

Vanda scrambled to stand. 'I didn't send Sorina – that was Una's doing.'

'The girl's no good at cleaning. But still…' He stopped then said, 'It will be for Edith to do after the wedding. Go and wash yourself. There's pig blood on your ugly face.'

Vanda stared at the butcher and wished she was a man for she would have killed him. If she had a gun, she would have shot him.

'Go home, bitch.' He pushed her until she was flattened against the tall yard gate. His eyes closed, a smile on his lips, he put his hands round her neck and tightened his grip. The gate shuddered and he sprang back as Vanda slumped to the ground.

'Who's there?' said the butcher.

'The mayor – I want a word about the wedding.'

With one hand the butcher lifted Vanda to her feet.

'Get out,' he whispered, opening the gate.

Gasping for breath, she pushed past the mayor and set off in the snow. Finding herself too weak to reach her home, she went reluctantly to the cabinet maker's house and opened the door. The cabinet maker was pulling on his boots and stood up so abruptly at the sight of Vanda that his chair fell over.

'How could you, you stinking drunk, agree to this marriage?' she said.

The cabinet maker, seeing the blood on her face and thinking her injured, did the only sensible thing: he retrieved his hat and scurried away.

'You rat,' she shouted after him.

Edith came out of her room, took one look at Vanda and fetched a bowl of water and a cloth.

'I'm not hurt. Leave me be, don't fuss,' said Vanda, sitting at the table. 'I just need to get my breath back, that's all.'

Edith put a firm hand on Vanda's forehead and wiped the blood from her face. Vanda didn't resist. Then she silently began to sob.

'If Misha is lost,' she said, 'there's so much I've never told him. I've never said I loved him and now it's too late.' She hung her head. 'All these years I've been so angry and it wasn't his fault. It was my father I should have... but I couldn't...'

Edith sat next to her and poured a glass of wine.

'I don't drink,' said Vanda as she lifted the glass to her mouth. She took out a handkerchief and blew her nose then looked at Edith. 'My father is a monster,' she said.

'There now. I've told you. That's what you're marrying.' She laughed to herself. 'It's not funny.' She glared at Edith who wasn't laughing. 'A monster. Do you want to know more?'

Edith stayed still, her eyes never leaving Vanda's face. She had a feeling that any sudden movement would scare away Vanda's words and once lost she doubted they would ever be heard.

'My mother died when I was sixteen. She was a weak woman. After years of abuse, I think she just gave up the ghost.' Vanda stared at the stove. 'I'm older than my sister by two years. After Mother's death I was expected to run the house, take over her role. My father rewarded me with my own bedroom. So it began. Every night he came to me. I couldn't stop him. I lived in dread of his step on the stairs, I knew what it meant. He told me I'd asked for it, that it was what I'd wanted. It lasted for two years. Two years of hell. I've never told a soul, not even my sister. I did all in my power to protect Una. I prayed that he never touched her. And then I realised I was pregnant. He found me a husband, the cobbler, and I married him on the understanding that my sister would marry the baker, and so it was.

'My husband never said a word when I gave birth four months later. I was spilt open so that the baby could be pulled from me feet first. I remember I looked at him and wished he was dead. But for a reason I don't understand, Misha chose to live. I felt nothing for him. I wouldn't let my husband touch me after that. But he's been a good father to Misha, a good husband to me.'

She paused. 'I did everything to keep my sister from him, only for her to be careless with her own daughter. And do you remember what she said when I told her about the hunting party? "Men will be men." That's all. But it wasn't all.' She stopped again. 'Could I have a little more?' Edith refilled her glass. 'You must have heard the gossip about your shepherd.'

Edith felt her stomach turn over. She was afraid of what she was about to hear but still she didn't look away.

'The men in the inn joke that my father killed him. I wouldn't put it past him.'

Edith's eyes filled with tears and Vanda reached across the table and took her hand. 'Surely what I've said has made you find your tongue? You honestly can't speak?'

Edith shook her head.

'Your stitchwork is some of the finest in the village. It always has been. And as for your painting, you are an artist.' Vanda still held Edith's hand. 'I've never told anyone what I've told you. Not a doctor, not a priest. Now, nearly too late, perhaps far too late, I realise that I married a good man, a kind man who has put up with me for eighteen years. My son is a good boy. I think hell has a special place for women like me. Thank you,' she said. 'Thank you for listening.'

Edith glanced up at a knock on the door. She opened it and found the cobbler there holding a pair of boots.

'I think these are your size, Edith,' he said. 'And no, I don't want any money. They're a wedding gift.'

He looked past Edith and was surprised to see his wife sitting calmly at the table.

'Vanda?' he said.

She stood and turned to him. 'Take me home,' she said.

# CHAPTER TWENTY

## THE EVE OF THE WEDDING

The cabinet maker had already taken the pig to be slaughtered for the wedding feast. Edith had wept to see it go as she had enjoyed the animal's company far more than her father's.

As was the custom the Sunday afternoon before a wedding, six young men of the village went from house to house striking pots and pans and knocking on every door with the cry of 'Bring cream'. This summons meant that each household was honour-bound to contribute to the wedding feast and every gift was rewarded by a glass of wine. In normal times this would be an occasion for celebration but there was nothing ordinary about this winter or this wedding. A glass of wine did little to lessen the anxiety felt by everyone.

Tradition dictated that the bride's future mother-in-law would oversee the cooking of the wedding feast. In place of the mother-in-law, Una arrived early with Sorina. Edith let them in then took up her seat by the window and resolutely watched the snow falling, refusing all requests to help.

Lena arrived shortly afterwards to hear Una shouting at Edith.

'If this is the way you are going to run my father's house you will have short shrift from him.'

'What are you shouting about?' asked Lena.

'Look at her,' said Una pointing at Edith. Then seeing Lena was alone asked, 'Where's your mother?'

'At home,' said Lena.

Flora arrived next. She went to Edith and laid a hand on her shoulder.

Vanda was the last.

'You're late,' said Una. 'It sets a bad example, if I may say so.'

'Example,' repeated Vanda, weighing up the word. 'Example of what? We are in the middle of a disaster. This wedding isn't right. Two people have died, my son is still missing, and there isn't enough food or fuel to last the winter. What happens if illness strikes us? We'll all be dead for there's no way out of this place. So what example are we talking about?'

'Calm yourself,' said Una.

'No, Una,' said Flora. 'Vanda is right. We shouldn't be calm – we should all be angry.'

'We can't spare the food, but we have no choice,' said Flora. 'Edith has no voice and no say in the matter, and still we must cook. Because that's what's done, it's tradition.'

'Tradition forced on us by cruel husbands and bullies, unwise men – and unwise women,' said Lena. 'My mother couldn't see that the marks on me weren't a sign of my husband's love – but a sign of his resentment.'

The women looked at one another, shocked that they had all spoken so unguardedly.

Sorina too spoke up. 'It was the cuckoo that said "Yes" at the betrothal supper, not Edith. I don't ever want to get married, men are revolting. They make you dirty and you can't get clean again.'

'Where did you get that nonsense from?' asked her mother.

Vanda's face had lost its colour. She stared at Sorina.

'Well?' said Una sharply.

'My grandfather,' said Sorina.

Vanda sat down slowly.

Una gave her daughter a slap. 'You will show respect for your elders and betters. Do you hear me? Or do you want another one?'

Edith got up and stood between Una and her daughter.

'Out of my way, Edith,' said Una, raising her hand. Edith caught her arm and moved her towards the door. 'I'm not leaving – let go of my arm.' Edith opened the door onto the verandah, and a chill filled the room. Una pulled her arm free. 'There,' she said and started to busy herself.

'You've been asked to leave, Una,' said Vanda.

'Are you taking her side?' said her sister.

Vanda's voice was weary. 'Just go home – you're not wanted.'

Una picked up her basket. 'Come, Sorina, we're leaving.'

Sorina moved to her aunt's side. Una, realising she had no

support, went red. 'I'll tell our father about this. And what you all said.' She turned to Edith. 'I hate to think how he'll punish you, but he will punish you.' She opened the door and stepped out onto the verandah.

It was too much for Vanda. 'That's what women like you do,' she called after her. 'You help men like our father. You say men will be men – what does that mean for women? Will women be women? No, because when we are, we're too loud. We're told to be silent.'

'I don't know what you're talking about,' said Una. 'I'm sorry about Misha but...'

'Don't you dare say another word,' said Vanda.

'All I'm saying is that since the avalanche, sister, you haven't been yourself. Perhaps you, like our father, have been bewitched by this silent...'

'No,' said Vanda. 'That's not what tragedy does to you. I haven't been bewitched. I've been heard.'

Edith closed the door on Una.

'I will tell him, I will,' shouted Una.

Edith took up her seat by the window and Sorina sat beside her. In silence they watched Una plodding through the snow to her father's house. Edith could almost see her emitting lightning flashes of indignant rage. The butcher obviously had not wanted to hear what she had to say as a few minutes later she was trudging in the opposite direction.

When Sorina was certain that her mother had gone home, she whispered to Edith, 'Grandpa has your boots.'

\*

By mid-morning, a purpose of sorts had taken hold.

'If your grandmother was here, Edith, she'd tell us a story,' said Vanda.

'If her grandmother was here none of this would be happening,' said Flora.

The women were surprised when the door opened and Georgeta, the mayor's wife, stood there, tall and awkward. The room went quiet.

'I've brought food and wine,' she said to Edith who went to greet her. 'A wedding gift.' She clumsily put her basket on the table.

Edith wondered what the mayor's wife could possibly want. The basket of food struck her as an excuse rather than a present.

'Your grandmother was a good friend to me,' she said to Edith.

Still, no one had said a word. Georgeta's white face blushed, and Edith knew what she was thinking – that she shouldn't have come, that she was too tall, she was out of place and the only woman there not wearing traditional clothes. Edith indicated the rocking chair by the fire. Georgeta perched on the edge of the seat, and everyone waited for her to speak.

'Last night,' she said, 'I dreamed of Edith's grandmother and a story she told, but I can't remember the ending.' Then, seeing all the faces staring at her, she stood. 'This is most insensitive of me. I'll go. I'm sorry to have interrupted your work. This is not the moment for stories… ridiculous, it was a…' and more to herself, she said, '…a foolish, foolish…'

'I was just saying that a story is what we're missing,' said Vanda.

'Oh no,' said Georgeta, 'I'm no storyteller. I'm not even sure how to start it.'

'Start it like Edith's grandmother used to,' said Lena. 'It was what once took place…' She paused.

Georgeta took a deep breath. '…And if it had never been, it would not be told.'

'Louder,' Vanda said. 'We all want to hear.'

The snow badgered the windows as Georgeta started again, her words finding courage. 'Once, when the bloodless were as common as blades of grass and the world of otherness was known to man, there lived a wizard, wise, wiser beyond the spinning of the world, who travelled great distances and called himself a shepherd of man.' She stopped. 'Do you remember this story, Edith?'

Edith shook her head.

'Go on,' said Vanda. 'We're all listening.'

'One day,' Georgeta began to rock, the chair's rhythm giving pace to her telling, 'the wizard came to a village high up in the mountains, and there he saw a beautiful young girl. She had eyes as dark as his, and in her left eye he caught a reflection of his soul, and in her right eye he caught a reflection of hers.

'He said to her, "Tell me, what should a man value the most?" And without the loss of a heartbeat, she said, "Love."

'Then she asked him, "What should a man fear the most?" And without the loss of a heartbeat, the wizard said, "Greed, because it leads to envy, it leads to war, it leads to all that the devil feasts upon."

'"Then love is the greater. Love has compassion, love heals."

'The wizard was a handsome young man. He called to the stars, and from them he gave her a ring and asked if she would marry him. The village elders disapproved. They said she couldn't marry a man who wasn't from their region unless he could show himself worthy of her hand. Only if he tamed the mountain dragon would she be his bride.

'The wizard asked where the dragon was to be found. "In the lake, high up in the mountain," they said. This dragon was the cause of all the thunderstorms, hail and snow that plagued their crops and damaged their houses.

'The wizard said a sad farewell to his love and climbed the mountain, never to be seen again. The girl's heart broke. Her father, seeing that the wizard wasn't coming back, found her another suitor to marry her. He was grey and rich with a belly that a pig would be proud of.'

'How does the story end?' Sorina interrupted. 'With a wedding to the suitor with a pig's belly?'

'That's the problem, I'm not sure,' said Georgeta. 'I think it goes... on her wedding day...'

'On her wedding day...' And it was her grandmother's

voice that Edith heard as Georgeta rocked in her chair. '...A small white bird perched on the girl's windowsill and said to her, "Come away with me, and I will take you to the wizard. He is being held prisoner by the dragon, but once the beast sees what love is, its temper will be quelled."

'When the girl's father came to take her to the church, he found her bedroom empty. Although the villagers searched high and low, she was never seen again. Shortly afterwards the thunder ceased, and it was said that the dragon disappeared to the bottom of the lake and there he sleeps to this day. But where the wizard and his bride are, nobody knows.'

'There was no wedding, then?' said Sorina.

'Edith's grandmother said some stories are neither sad nor happy. In the telling, they are just what they are.'

That is so, thought Edith, and in this story, she saw more than a glimmer of hope. She saw it was her grandmother's wedding gift to her, brought by the mayor's wife.

'I should be leaving,' said Georgeta. 'It will soon be dark.'

*

The mayor was at home in his study, smoking his pipe. He had long been contemplating a letter from a merchant who was concerned about his son who he had last heard from in the spring when he'd written to tell his parents he was to marry a village girl called Edith. The mayor knew he should have done something when Demetrius didn't return to the village but he hadn't. The butcher had got the better of him.

If the mayor was honest – a quality the merchant's letter now demanded – he'd been frightened of the butcher ever since they were young. The son of a butcher, even as a boy he'd been stronger, bigger than other lads his age. He was a fighter and the mayor had been his punch bag.

Since they'd become men, the mayor's comfort had been that he was better educated, richer and more powerful than the butcher. But last summer his confidence had been shattered on the night of the hunting party. The innkeeper had sent for him when a troubling incident occurred. The mayor had been greeted at the inn door by the butcher.

'Go home,' he'd said. 'This is none of your business.'

'I'm here to enforce the law.'

A smile had momentarily flickered across the butcher's thin lips. The mayor shuddered to think of it.

'By all means come in and rattle that chain of office,' he'd said, 'if you want me to tell the elders about your son.'

'My son?' said the mayor.

'Yes, your son. What I know about him would ruin you.'

'I don't know what you're talking about.'

'I'd tell you but I don't want to sully my mouth. You'll receive a package of letters tomorrow.'

'What letters?' said the mayor. His stomach churned.

'Letters I found when I helped dig out the bodies at the house of the miller's son. So are you coming in?'

'I was called here by the innkeeper,' said the mayor.

The butcher stepped back, opening the door wide. 'Then you must do what you must do. And I'll do what I must do.'

The mayor didn't move. The butcher went back inside the inn and closed the door.

The mayor stood outside, shaking at his own impotence. He was trying to compose himself when from an open window of the inn he heard the butcher then the slurred voice of a drunken young man.

'So you know where to find my brother?' said the young man. 'Can you take me there?'

The mayor now regretted he hadn't stayed to hear the butcher's reply.

Dazed, he had gone home.

In the morning the package had been brought to him by his maid.

'The butcher said to tell you there are more where those came from,' she said. 'He thought you should know, sir.' She'd bobbed a curtsy and left him to open the package.

He'd seen that the three letters were clearly written in his son's hand. Love letters – and for a moment he'd felt relief. No harm in a boy of his age having an affair. He'd read the second letter and turned to the third when he stopped. For the first time he saw who they were addressed to. It made no sense. The love letters were addressed to the miller's son. At the end of each the mayor's son begged that he burn it so it wouldn't fall into the wrong hands.

The mayor had laughed mirthlessly at that. If this matter should ever come to light the consequences were too terrible to contemplate. His position, his reputation, the family name would be ruined. His son would not graduate, would not practise law. With every thought the mayor felt himself one step closer to the precipice. It would take only a careless word and he would fall.

Since then he'd been unable to exert his authority over the butcher or, for that matter, the priest.

Sons, he thought now, reading the merchant's letter again. And again he felt powerless. He went to the window to close the curtains. This should be done for me, he thought, would be done, if all the women weren't cooking for this farce of a wedding. He had his hands on the heavy fabric when he looked out. He couldn't think what his wife was doing standing outside the house, staring up the road.

*

Lena, who was dusting the cabinet maker's parlour, had a good view of the street. Her cry brought all the women rushing to the window.

The cobbler was mending the butcher's cuckoo clock. He stepped out for some fresh air and thought he was seeing a ghost. Nevertheless, he ran towards it.

Thin, bearded but defiantly alive, Misha was pulling a makeshift sleigh down the icy street.

Vanda was the first out of the door. She ran to her son, blind to the sleigh and its cargo. Edith, close behind her, saw only the body of Demetrius lying on the sleigh, his violin on his chest. She fell to her knees. In his frozen fingers was her gold coin.

# CHAPTER TWENTY-ONE

## THE DARK STAIN

Edith heard herself cry out, a wordless sound that came from the depth of all that was broken in her. The absence of Demetrius, of his soul in the world, of his love for her, overwhelmed her. Snow, in all its forgetfulness, had buried him, flake by gentle flake. And only when the mountain gods roared had they remembered their buried treasure and reluctantly returned him. A wedding gift.

A crowd of people had come out of their houses to stare. From behind his shuttered windows, the butcher was watching.

'Misha will pay for this,' he said under his breath. 'Yes, he will pay.'

Edith's limbs had lost their strength. Flora, Lena and Sorina gathered round her. She couldn't think why they were there. For a moment there was only the past, no future, the present a gaping wound.

'I knew I would find him,' said Misha. 'We'll take him to the blacksmith.'

In the failing light, a small procession of women followed the sleigh as Misha pulled it to the forge. The news had already reached the blacksmith and he walked out to meet it. Together, he and Misha carried Demetrius' body into the house and laid it on a wooden table.

'He will be given his last rites later,' said the blacksmith, taking the violin.

'Do you want to be left alone with him?' Misha asked Edith.

Edith nodded.

The door grated on the floor as the blacksmith pulled it to. A candle in a metal holder sat on the windowsill, a draught causing the light to flicker across Demetrius' face. He looked peaceful, a smile on his lips. Edith rested her hand on his frozen fingers. She bent and kissed him.

*'What happened to you?'*

There was only the silence of the dead.

Edith felt her soul shaking as if grief would loosen it from its earthly moorings. When she saw her reflection in the window, she realised it was dark. There were voices outside the room, and the blacksmith appeared at the door and showed in the mayor. Behind him were the doctor and the priest. The mayor shook his head, or so Edith thought. Edith longed for words.

'It's best that you leave now, Edith,' said the mayor. 'Go home. I'm sure there's much to do for tomorrow.'

Edith stared at him defiantly.

'We must examine the body,' said the doctor. 'Without you here,' he added sharply and summoned Vanda who had been waiting in another room.

She took Edith's arm, but Edith brushed it away and shook her head.

'We'll stay,' said Vanda. 'If it's all the same to you.'

'Women,' the priest muttered under his breath.

The doctor took off his jacket, hung it over a chair and rolled up his sleeves. Strange, thought Edith, how these details, these unimportant gestures take on such significance. She sensed that the three men were dreading what they might find.

The doctor examined Demetrius – his face, his chest. 'There's no sign of a wound,' he said, barely touching the shepherd's clothes.

'You should turn him over, Doctor,' the blacksmith said, coming into the room. 'You take his legs, and I the head… gently now.'

Something clattered onto the stone floor and all the men jumped. Edith's gold coin had come free from Demetrius' fingers and rolled across the room.

The mayor picked it up. 'You should give this to the butcher tomorrow.'

'How can you be so insensitive?' said Vanda as Edith took the coin from him. They turned the shepherd like a log, face down, his arms frozen to his sides. There was a gasp of disbelief from the men, and for a moment Edith couldn't understand what she was seeing. On Demetrius' back was a dark stain.

'My God,' said the mayor. 'He was shot – in the back.'

Edith felt her knees weaken. The room spun, and she nearly fell.

'Take her away,' said the doctor, his voice harsh. 'Get her out of here.'

But Edith refused to move.

'Quiet,' said the blacksmith. 'The dead deserve respect. Let's turn him again.'

Edith placed the coin where once Demetrius' heart beat.

She kept her hand there and stared with fury at the mayor, at the doctor, at the priest. All corrupt, she thought, and in the palm of the butcher's hand. She thought of her grandmother's story – what should a man fear the most? Greed, because it leads to envy, it leads to war, it leads to all that the devil feasts upon.

'The gold coin belongs to Demetrius,' said Vanda, 'the man Edith was engaged to, whom she loved.' She put her arm around Edith. 'You, Mayor, should stop this wedding. 'Or are you afraid of my father, too?'

*

The mayor poured himself a brandy to steady his nerves.

'Is there anything you need, sir?' asked the maid.

He shook his head and dismissed her.

'Is there anything I need?' he said to himself. Yes, to

not have the shepherd's body lying at the blacksmith's house with a bullet in his back. He washed his hands in a basin, checked his beard in the mirror and thought himself well suited to the role he had been given. He sat behind his desk, knowing that it gave him more authority. He smelled the elders before they had entered his study, their clothes musty with a faint whiff of camphor. He reached in a drawer for a small bottle of cologne and dabbed it on his beard.

The maid knocked and opened the door for the elders, the doctor, the priest and the cabinet maker. They made the mayor's study seem small. And Misha was there. Why the cursed boy should have chosen this of all days to bring the body down from the mountain, he couldn't imagine. He should have left it up there until after his grandfather's wedding. But he was the village idiot. The mayor cleared his throat.

'Before the avalanche, I received a letter from the shepherd's father. He is a merchant in the town. He wrote because he'd had no word from his son who he knew was engaged to a girl called Edith who lives in this village.'

The word 'merchant' surprised the cabinet maker.

'Are you sure?' he said. 'I thought the shepherd was a gypsy.'

'As I said, he was a merchant's son.'

The cabinet maker, never able to keep his thoughts to himself, said aloud, 'Wealthy?'

'I would imagine so.'

The cabinet maker felt the icy gaze of the butcher on him and said, quickly, but with a hint of regret, 'It was a passing whim of Edith's – just a girlish crush.'

The mayor continued. 'The merchant asked me to make enquiries.'

'It seems that Misha made enquiries for you,' said the butcher taking charge of the situation, 'so the mystery is solved.'

'Quite so,' mumbled the other elders.

'Not so hasty,' said the mayor. 'Let the doctor speak.'

'Perhaps,' said the doctor, 'we should discuss this at a later date.'

'Agreed,' said the butcher. 'Tomorrow is my wedding.'

The mayor tried to regain control. 'It's precisely because of the wedding that this must be discussed now. There is a feeling among the womenfolk that the marriage should wait. Doctor, please continue.'

'The young man was killed by a bullet in the back from what I believe was a hunting gun.'

The men muttered to each other in shock and disbelief.

The mayor interrupted them. 'I'm sure you'll all agree that in these circumstances, the wedding is… ah… inadvisable.'

No one spoke. All eyes were on the butcher.

'What?' he said. 'Let all the food go to waste? The pigs and the chickens, all butchered for nothing? Tomorrow I'm going to be married. It makes no difference if the blacksmith has two or three bodies unburied. The earth is hard, so the matter can wait.'

The mayor felt the blood in him rise but, at the very same moment, a cooling thought came to him. He could not afford to be on the wrong side of this man.

'Surely there is no doubt that the young man was murdered,' he said.

'Murdered?' said the butcher. 'Says who?' He brought his fist down on the desk, causing the mayor's papers to dance and his paperweight to rock. The nerve-shattering sound reminded the men of the avalanche and the power of the mountain they perched on. The butcher turned away from the mayor and spoke directly to the assembled company. 'How many here have hunting guns?'

Every man in the room reluctantly raised his hand, except Misha. The gun he'd secretly bought was a revolver.

'It must have been an accident,' said the butcher. 'Perhaps,' he leaned menacingly on the mayor's desk, 'it was you. You were a bad shot when you were young. I don't imagine you to be any better in old age.'

'But why would anyone go hunting so high up?' said the miller.

'I wondered that myself,' said Misha, speaking for the first time. 'And the shepherd wasn't wearing his boots. I think whoever murdered him hoped the wolves would eat the corpse.'

The uneasy silence was broken by the butcher. 'Are you going to listen to the opinion of the village idiot?'

Misha stood tall. He had been on the mountain night and day in the most inhospitable weather. He had stared his fear in the face, and the mountain gods had kept him strong. No man was going to say his word wasn't to be trusted.

'I'm no idiot,' he said. 'I know exactly where I found the body and I think none of us here would be surprised by whose gun fired the bullet.'

'Are you accusing me of murder?' said the butcher.

Misha said, 'You alone know the truth of what you did.'

'The marriage should wait,' said the mayor decisively.

The butcher looked round the room at every man there, each of them trying to avoid his eye. 'There's no proof the shepherd was murdered. If you choose to believe the word of this idiot, what then? I'll tell you. I hope you all have enough food stored for the winter because if my wedding doesn't go ahead tomorrow, I will not lift a finger to help anyone in trouble. Do you understand what that means?'

There was silence.

'I've no objection to the wedding,' said the cabinet maker quickly. 'And my daughter is ready.'

One of the elders spoke up. 'The chief elder has a point. The investigation, if there is to be one, should take place when spring arrives and the constable can be brought from the town. But meanwhile, life must go on.'

The other elders and the doctor agreed.

The priest said, 'I give the wedding my blessing.'

The butcher turned to the mayor.

'Then tomorrow I will be married.'

'You should all be ashamed of yourselves,' said Misha. 'You are forcing a wedding on a woman who has lost the man she truly loved.'

'Idiot,' said the butcher as Misha left the room. Then, turning to the mayor, said, 'What about a drink?'

Georgeta was in the hall looking even paler than usual. 'Misha,' she said, 'you are not, and you never have been, an idiot.'

# CHAPTER TWENTY-TWO

## THE ALCHEMY OF MUSIC

That night the sky was clear and the stars rested on top of the mountain. An eerie hush gripped the village. The community was holding its breath, waiting to see what would happen now that the shepherd's body had been found.

'Is the wedding still going ahead?' Vanda asked Georgeta when she arrived at the cabinet maker's house.

'I'm afraid it is,' said Georgeta and told the women all she had overheard.

'It's as I thought. He was murdered,' said Vanda. 'By my father.'

The women were quiet.

'My husband is a weak man,' said Georgeta. 'They are all weak men – except for your son. You would have been proud to hear him stand up to your father.'

She went to Edith who was sitting alone. 'My husband had a letter from a merchant in town, enquiring after his son,' she said, quietly. 'The merchant had last heard from him when he wrote to say he was engaged to a girl from this village called Edith.'

Edith had long expected this day and now it was here. There was no light, there was no darkness, no definition. Grief had no edge to it. She was lost. Words were pebbles that skimmed the flat, tideless water of sorrow.

'A merchant family,' Georgeta was saying. 'If the mayor had known he would have raised a search party.'

Edith closed her eyes. She had long known her love was dead. She had known instinctively, just as she knew she would never be the butcher's wife.

It was while Flora and Maria were helping Edith to get dressed that evening that Edith remembered her grandmother's coat. A coat of fables she called it. Edith had long kept it safe at the bottom of her hope box for she and her grandmother had embroidered it with her grandmother's many stories. She spread it out on the bed.

'It's beautiful,' said Flora.

Edith put it on. The coat was heavy, the weight of it comforting. It was too large and trailed on the floor but she looked magical in it.

Vanda said, 'If we had eyes to see the dead, I believe we'd see your grandmother here with us.'

Edith believed Demetrius was there too, even though she couldn't hear him in her head, even though she couldn't see him. She was confident that he stood beside her.

The women of the village began to arrive at the bride's house, as was the tradition. The men went to the butcher's house to drink the health of the bridegroom. There would have been more joy at a funeral than there was at these two gatherings. None of the talk was of the wedding, all was of the murder. Every man thought he knew who the killer was but daren't say his name; every woman said quietly, 'The butcher.'

Edith sat where she had when the day began, before she knew what the hours held. The glow of the candle reflected in the window behind her gave her a golden halo of light. Georgeta thought she had an unearthly quality, that her spirit was on the edge of a journey.

Edith watched the women come in, take wine and cakes and try not to stare at her. They whispered, their low voices a swarm of sleepy bees. Una came with Lena's mother and was careful to avoid her sister.

What can I do, thought Edith, closing her eyes. What would I say if I had a voice? I would tell the butcher, 'No,' and still he wouldn't hear. How many women in this room had ever been heard, for all their talking?

Una, with determined cheerfulness, lifted her glass to drink a toast to the bride.

'Come, Vanda,' she said. 'It's the tradition. Here's to happiness and a long life.'

Vanda put down her glass and she shook her head. 'No, this is not a celebration where we all come together, remember our weddings and make the bride blush about the loss of her innocence. This is a wake. A young man who Edith willingly gave her gold coin – her heart – to has been murdered.'

'Sister,' hissed Una. 'It was a hunting accident.'

Silence fell over the gathering and Vanda was about to say more when there was a knock on the door. Lena opened it and found Misha, washed and shaved. She slipped out for a moment to speak to him and came back a little flushed.

'Tell him to go away,' called Una. 'It's unlucky for a man to be here.'

'He wants a word with his mother,' said Lena.

Vanda wrapped her shawl round her and went onto the verandah. 'Are you going to your grandfather's house?' she asked.

'No,' said Misha. 'Neither is Father. I'm going to spend the evening with him. I wanted Edith to have this.' He held up the violin and bow. 'I've polished it but I don't know how to tune it.' He gave it to his mother and turned to go.

Vanda reached out and caught her son's hand. The look of surprise on his face shocked her.

'Wait,' she said. 'I just…'

'What is it, Mother?' Misha asked.

'I want to tell you that I am sorry for the way I've been towards you, truly sorry. You are a far better son than I deserve.'

'On the mountain I thought about a lot of things,' said Misha. 'And I think the way you were was not your fault.'

He touched her arm and for once she didn't brush him away.

'I couldn't have lived with myself if you'd died up there,' she said and in the moonlight he saw a miracle of sorts take place. His mother's face filled with love for him, the hard lines softened by her tears.

'I love you, Mother,' he said.

Vanda wiped her eyes with the back of her hand. 'And I you,' she said. 'And I you.'

She took the violin and bow from him, went indoors and gave them to Edith.

Edith ran her finger over the violin. I have no way to tell of my grief, my anger, she said silently to herself. I have no voice. Be my voice.

She put the violin under her chin and with the bow played a note. It cut across the conversation; the room became quiet. Edith tightened the strings.

'I think it will take practice,' said Flora gently.

Again Edith put the violin under her chin. She closed her eyes and started to play. This is my voice, she told herself. I will speak in music. And so the first chord rose; a long wailing note that climbed to infinity then a rush of quick, urgent notes, jiggering and giddy. There was a long pause, and no one in the room dared breathe, for this was surely unearthly sorcery. Edith started to play again. The music spiralled upwards and with a sigh fell into a whisper until a tune broke free and danced its rage, its sorrow, its heartbreak into the starry sky. The older women stared at Edith in speechless wonder; the young women wept for all that they could have been, for all that had been stolen from them, for the injustice of lives ruled by fools. The alchemy of the music soared out of the cabinet maker's house, and Edith's wordless lament was heard throughout the village. It reached the butcher's ears and stung his blackened heart.

# CHAPTER TWENTY-THREE

## SNOW SONG

Edith heard the tinkling of bells, the sound of Demetrius bringing his sheep down from the mountain. She woke with regret, knowing it was a dream.

She lay half asleep, but still she heard the gentle chimes. Now wide awake, she rose and opened her shutters. Snow was falling yet the sky was pink, shot through with blues; such an unnatural morning sky. She laughed as she realised it was the snowflakes making the music of the heavens.

Edith dressed and opened her bedroom door. Her father was snoring in a chair by the stove. She walked softly past him, whereupon he jumped to his feet.

'Where are you going?' he said, and cursed his sudden movement. His head hurt and it sounded as if pots and pans were falling all round his ears. 'What's that terrible noise?' Then as Edith opened the door, he said, 'No, I'll do it. I'll feed the hens.'

Amused, she followed him onto the verandah. She put out her hand and caught a perfect snowflake.

'Don't stand there, girl,' said her father. 'Go inside, it's freezing.'

She realised why he'd been sleeping in the chair: he was frightened she would run away. Where could she run to? If she'd had somewhere to go, she would have left long ago. Her idea was far more brutal. There are other ways to go travelling, she told herself, even if the destination is unknown.

The coffee was on the table along with the bread, butter and jam and still the cabinet maker hadn't come back. She wrapped her shawl round her and went onto the verandah and watched the snow. This was the snow song that storytellers of old had spoken of. Her grandmother had said that those who were innocent thought it was the music of the heavens, those who were guilty heard the devil's pots and pans falling.

'The hens are all gone,' said her father. 'Every one of them. Can't you hear the noise? It must've frightened them away.'

Edith went back into the house and opened her grandmother's room.

'Do you think a fox got them all?' he said, stamping the snow from his boots.

A hen waddled up to him and another flew onto the table. 'How did they get in here?' Receiving no reply, he said, 'I need a drink,' and disappeared into his room.

The yard gate opened, and Edith was nearly blinded by

a flash of light from the mirror the blacksmith was carrying. Flora was almost dancing as she came in.

'I never thought I would live to hear the snow sing,' she said. 'Can you hear it?'

Edith nodded.

'I thought you should see yourself – we'll put the mirror in your room.'

When the blacksmith had propped up the mirror, Edith touched his coat and put her hand to her ear.

'What do I hear? I hear bells, a flock of sheep,' he said. 'I'm sorry about the shepherd,' he added as he left.

'I know you're going to wear traditional costume,' Flora said, unpacking her basket, 'but I thought you should have this. It's my wedding present to you.'

The white bird, thought Edith as Flora hung the dress on the bedroom door. Edith had never seen such a lovely garment, elegant yet simple in its design. The feel of the fabric spoke of another life. She smiled. This is the dress I'm going to wear, she thought, the one the butcher promised me, a dress to fly away in. She pointed to the dress and then to herself.

Flora said, 'But what will the elders say?' and laughed when she saw Edith's face. 'Then, my lady, I shall dress you. And stuff and nonsense to the rest. Perhaps,' she added, 'a little plum wine for us wouldn't go amiss.'

By the time the church bells rang out over the village, a few of the older women had gathered at the cabinet maker's house to light the fire, lay out the food and shoo the hens into the yard.

Flora had just finished dressing Edith's white hair with handmade white flowers when Georgeta called in on her way to the church. 'Edith,' she said, kissing her cheek, 'if your grandmother was here she would say you are the Snow Queen from one of her tales.'

Edith slipped her feet into a pair of delicate satin shoes and Flora turned round the mirror so that she could see herself. Edith didn't recognise the woman she was looking at, a woman with wisdom in her eyes and an hypnotic gaze. Was this her? She had wondered if the loss of her voice had made her invisible, but now she saw there was nothing weak in her. Yes, she said to herself, I have strength enough to do this.

Flora said, 'You are the most beautiful woman I have ever dressed.'

Edith picked up the violin and the bow and held them as if they were a bouquet.

'Good luck,' said Georgeta as she set off to the church.

The old women stared open-mouthed when Edith walked into the kitchen.

'Are we ready?' said her father, swaying somewhat. There were two Ediths and neither of them – or perhaps one of them – was dressed in traditional costume. He looked again. 'But... you're not... that's the white wedding dress. You're not...'

Edith stared at him, her eyes blazing with determination. She could see that her father was weighing up the arguments.

'Change,' he commanded. 'Go and change. And give me

that violin.' Edith shook her head, and her father, defeated by alcohol and a daughter he didn't know, said, 'All right. It doesn't matter a bear's shirt as long as you're married. Let the butcher – let your husband – punish you. Not me. We should be going... yes, we should be going. I've forgotten something... what is it?'

What indeed, thought Edith, who had suspected all along that her father had forgotten to do what the butcher had requested: arrange a sleigh to take them to the church. Now there was nothing for it other than to go on foot. Edith went back into her bedroom and changed her shoes for the hardy boots the cobbler had given her. Flora carried the satin slippers.

'You can put them on at the church,' she said, picking up the train of the wedding dress.

The cabinet maker clasped his daughter's arm in a vice-like grip. Edith held the violin and the bow under her other arm and they walked through the falling snow to the church.

The priest was waiting outside for them. The snow bothered him. The noise rang in his ears and he tried to brush it away. For a moment he wasn't sure what he was seeing; an angel seemed to be walking down the street.

Only when the cabinet maker said, 'We're here,' did the priest realise that Edith had defied the elders and was wearing the wedding dress. He turned on the cabinet maker. 'We would have been late if she'd...' And in trying to explain, the cabinet maker unintentionally let go of Edith's arm.

The butcher was waiting in the front pew. Vanda, Una,

Sorina and Misha sat behind him. The whole village had turned out for the ceremony. A whisper reached the butcher that Edith had arrived and was wearing the white wedding dress. The butcher felt a flash of anger but told himself it didn't matter. Soon, she would be his property. Under his jacket, he was wearing the red shirt that Edith had sewn and embroidered for her husband-to-be. He had ordered the cabinet maker to fetch it from her hope chest. But it had been made to fit Demetrius and the butcher had had to slit it up the back so he could button it. But at least he was dressed as a bridegroom should be.

The organ ground out its tuneless chords, and still there was no sign of the bride. The congregation began to fidget and then a cold wind whirled into the church. The organ music that had just finished started again and everyone rose to their feet, waiting for the bride to enter. Instead, the priest walked with determined steps to the altar followed by Flora and the now sober cabinet maker, beads of sweat on his forehead. He was much out of breath.

'I'm sorry,' said the cabinet maker to the butcher, 'Edith has run off. I'm sure she'll be back... I know she'll be back.'

*

The second her father had let go of her arm, Edith had picked up her skirt and ran. She ran as fast as she could, slip-sliding but never entirely falling. Behind her she could hear her father shouting, his voice trailing away on the icy breeze. On she ran towards the forest and she dared not look back.

Edith felt the mountain and its whalebone curve as she began to climb. It took all her energy to make progress. If she could reach the edge of the forest she stood a chance of staying hidden. Her dress white, the sky white, the snow white, all without shape, only the forest was a faint etching of dark grey lines on white paper. Still the snow fell.

*

All the breath in her was gone when she reached the forest. She rested her head on the trunk of a beech tree and listened to the wind. The snow was not so deep under the branches of the trees but she strayed off the path, tripped and found herself slipping down a bank, her foot going through ice into a stream, filling her boot with freezing water. Taking care not to damage the violin, she scrambled out and up the bank. The trees were close together and they caught her dress, and the thorny undergrowth, remembering its sharp claws, tore at her flesh. She was now buried in the forest, where day became night and only the snow, glinting with diamonds, lit the way. Where was she going, where could she hide, said a small voice in her. She turned at the sound of a hunting horn to see if she was being followed. There was no one. She went on, hoping her footprints would disappear under fresh snow before anyone came after her.

Finally, she reached the necklace of white-coated fir trees

that guarded the mountain itself and here the snow became deeper again, harder to walk in. Edith was weary and had lost track of time. She thought she heard dogs barking.

The light was beginning to disappear. There was little chance of her surviving, she'd known that when she started to run. She was ill-dressed for such a place and such weather and already she was so cold she could hardly feel her feet or fingers and it hurt to walk. It doesn't matter, she told herself, I'm the white bird flying free.

Now she heard the unmistakable voice of the butcher shouting her name.

'Edith!' Her name ricocheted from tree to tree.

She could see the lights of distant lanterns through the branches and knew there were more men with him. Holding tight to the violin and the bow she started to run as the sound of the dogs came ever nearer.

'Over there,' shouted the butcher.

She was too exhausted to go any faster. At that moment when she felt all was lost, she saw the outline of two fir trees standing close together. Covered in snow, in the twilight they looked like the skirts of dancing ladies, and without another thought, she pushed through them. She was in a tunnel of soft green branches, and suddenly she was through them and in a clearing. The light seemed brighter there, and a little way off stood a small dwelling in a sea of untouched snow. She went closer, called softly. There was no reply. The door was hanging off its hinges and inside snow dusted the floor. The place was derelict.

Edith had no more strength left in her. She sat on the floor, the violin in her lap, and waited. It wouldn't be long now until the butcher arrived. As she was thinking this, she became aware that she couldn't hear him calling and no dogs were barking. In the peaceful silence, darkness enveloped her and, shivering, she lay down, curled into a ball, the violin next to her. She closed her eyes and let sleep take her in its warm arms.

On the edge of dreaming, she heard a voice say, 'I am here, I am beside you.'

# CHAPTER TWENTY-FOUR

## WALKING BETWEEN
## TWO WORLDS

Edith sees her grandmother, a golden crown on her head. She sits cradling an ancient book. Words seep from its pages, letter by letter they free themselves from sentences.

'Busy little ants,' her grandmother says. 'The letters run away, taking the full stops with them.' She smiles at Edith. 'So you are here. Better get up. No good lying there tangled in that dress – unless you want to die. Do you want to die? Come on now, conjure yourself up.'

Edith has no voice to answer her.

'I can hear you all the same,' her grandmother says. 'You know this place. I told you of it many times – of its forest, of its cabin. Of the stranger who comes from far away and brings a different kind of magic. He is preparing you a feast.'

Should she be frightened?

'Stir your bones, girl, stir your bones.'

Edith kneels. It's dark but the light of the moon shows her a stove, a chair.

'There's wood,' she hears her grandmother say. 'And look, a dead man's coat made of good, warm wool.'

It's hard fighting sleep. All she wants to do is lie down again. It seems a long journey to the chair. Blind fingers, bone cold, she crawls across the floor until she collides with a mix of wooden legs and soft fabric. A coat, a chair. She laughs and puts the coat round her. It's lined with sheepskin, its smell familiar, comforting.

'Good with the needle was your love,' says her grandmother. 'Warmer now.'

It seems to Edith that her grandmother's words ignite the kindling in the stove and catches it alight.

The room begins to fill with a flock of bleating sheep, or so she imagines, and she can hardly see her grandmother. Counting the sheep, Edith falls asleep.

She wakes and thinks she's in a bed. Perhaps this bed is given to all silent women so they might rest awhile before they disappear into dust, their lives marked only by small graves, their footsteps hardly seen in the snow.

Her limbs are cold, ice fills the centre of her. She is lying on the floor. From here she takes in the cabin. At least it has a roof and two rooms, and the door is now shut firm against the outside world. Through the broken shutters the sun shines in a bright line across the floor. Last night the darkness felt as thick as velvet and she hadn't been able to see the whole cabin to know how big or small it was. There is a table, two chairs. Her hands shaking, she lights the stove and begins to explore every nook and cranny. There are storage jars filled with oats, barley, flour and dried pulses. Whoever lived here would not leave it with a larder this full.

In the other room is a bed with a mattress, a fur thrown across it. She wraps the fur round her. At the foot of the bed is a large chest, full of more furs, linens. There's a knife and a box with six needles, red thread, a thimble and a pair of scissors. Three boxes of candles. A flint box, a bar of soap. How strange – such luxuries to be abandoned. And she thinks, what does it matter? I'm wearing a wedding dress. I ran into a clearing, found a deserted cabin. I fell asleep on a frozen wooden floor.

Where would she want to be? Here or back in the village, married to the butcher? The thought makes her shudder. No, this place, this interlude, is to be relished, to be enjoyed. She is free here until death claims her.

Outside the snow glimmers, pink and purple. The forest, a dark impenetrable wall, surrounds her. She opens the door of the cabin to find two dead rabbits there, tied together with a bunch of herbs. The snow shows no sign of footprints. The forest, her grandmother would tell her, is where all healing stories come from and a stranger's kindness can save your life. Edith listens to the silence; there is no pulse of another life to it. The snow makes the world sleepy in its hibernation.

Edith spends the morning gathering kindling and bring-ing in the logs. She puts a battered pan on the stove, skins one of the rabbits and puts its long, pink body in the pan on the stove with the herbs and some barley. She smells it simmering, impatient for it to be cooked. Her stomach sings songs to the battered pan. To take her mind off food she goes out again to collect firewood and berries. She finds mushrooms, for if you dig under the snow the winter larder is still full and frozen.

When she's collected a basketful she returns to the cabin. She takes the pan to the table and hungrily sucks the tender flesh from the carcass. Never has a dish tasted as sweet. Sated and tired, she climbs under the fur in all her many layers and sleeps. She dreams that Demetrius is with her, his fingers touching hers.

He says, 'I knew you were a walker between two worlds.'

She thinks her voice might have returned. 'Where is your violin?' she asks. He points up and she sees it floating above his head.

Sunlight flickers across her eyelashes and throws soft shadows in the room. She props herself up. The wood-panelled walls are painted with a scene of mountains and forests and she can't remember if they were painted when she first saw the room. There are bears and, if you look, wolves and eagles. It seems to her that the shepherd and his sheep are moving from field to field. She wonders if this is Demetrius' doing, if it was he who left the rabbits. Had he watched over her while she was sleeping?

She wakes as it is getting dark, surprised she's slept so long. What a strange moon it is that shines on her tonight. She lights a candle and takes the rabbit bones out of the stock and puts them by the stove to dry. She makes a soup from what remains. It tastes so good. Sweet rabbit, thank you for your life.

The snow badgers the windows, rattles the door. She looks up and half expects to hear the stamp of Demetrius' feet, his voice saying, 'My love.' That night she stays close to the stove. When the bones are dry she lays them out on the table as if by reassembling the rabbit she might, as in one of her grandmother's stories, bring it back to life. They don't quite lie down, these bones that once hopped and jumped.

Edith puts the violin under her chin. It feels to her that an unseen hand guides the bow across the strings and plays a tune so infectious that she begins to dance. She dances until she is too hot in her coat. She takes it off and dances herself wild. She stops suddenly. She's heard something, someone. She puts down the bow and picks up the knife, her mind playing tricks in the dark. She waits and wonders if her playing might have brought the devil to her.

There is no one there. In the cupboard she finds plum brandy among some bottles and she pours a little into a cup. She takes a sip and then another.

This moment of consciousness is the beginning.

*

For a while, gifts are left for her – a pheasant, a hare, a partridge – and the snow always covers the tracks of whoever brought them. A part of her says Demetrius is beside her and she wonders at how he makes such magic happen. When the gifts cease to arrive she becomes a huntress. She makes a trap and catches a partridge; both she and the bird surprised at the audacity of her actions. Triumphant, she brings it home, kills it and plucks it. She saves the feathers to make a headdress.

*

She keeps the cabin warm; there are enough logs, enough food, and winter has bedded itself down. Edith wishes she could speak and tell Demetrius she isn't frightened. She would say, 'Whatever happens, I will be ready.'

She takes pieces of fur from the chest and makes a pattern for a hat. In the candlelight, close to the stove, she stitches.

*

Days fall into each other. The routine of life is ruled by the need for warmth and food. Sleep is a blessing. She has no concept of how much of winter has passed and how much is still to come. Some nights, curled up in the bed as the wind and snow whistle into the cabin, she sees herself hidden in a vast forest, part of a spinning world suspended in space. None of it matters and all of it matters. She becomes braver, stronger, growing into the unknown parts of herself that have always been there. It feels, she thinks, like finding your house has more rooms than you knew. She has become a hunter. She becomes a survivor.

The snow is falling and, wearing her hat, she builds a snowman and then a snowwoman to keep him company. In the forest she finds decoration for them until these visitors look almost real, then she silently addresses them as if they were her old friends.

'When will he be here?' she asks the snowwoman who wears an antler skull on her head.

'I saw him when your back was turned,' the snowwoman replies.

She asks the snowman with his rabbit hat, 'Does he see me?'

'He looked in your direction,' the snowman says.

She asks the snowwomen if he came searching for his violin.

'Yes, he put it under his chin to play you a lullaby but you were already asleep.'

This pretence near defeats her. She feels her longing for Demetrius as an ache inside her.

He is dead. I saw him dead. I know he is dead.

She crumbles into the snow. This one thought is all it takes to pull down her dreams and she is overwhelmed by a terrible sense of abandonment. What will she do? Go back down the mountain? Where would she go? Back to her village and the vengeance of the butcher?

She makes mushroom soup with the stock from a pheasant and goes to bed, hoping she'll dream of him.

\*

She dresses. A ray of weak sunshine turns the snow pink. She makes porridge from the oats and dreams of honey to sweeten it. Because I'm silent, it doesn't mean there are no words in me. You just can't hear me. Because I can't see you, it doesn't mean you're not here. I know you are. You are in everything that has kept me safe and given me a place of rest so I might gather the missing words.

*

The silence is shattered by the barking of dogs, the shouts of men, a barrage of sound that startles Edith's senses. She hears the rustle of trees, the thud of snow and in the clearing a bear cub stops, terrified, and cries into the forest. Even before Edith sees the huntsmen, she has one arm in the coat, and is half out of the cabin. Conscious only of the bear, the small vulnerable bear, she lifts the animal; the weight of the tiny creature causes her to stumble. She smells the forest in its fur, smells its fear. She straightens and turns back to the cabin, the little bear clinging to its rescuer.

Two huntsmen appear in the clearing, their guns levelled at her.

One of them, who has a feather in his hat, shouts, 'Put it down. It's our kill. A fair chase. Put the bear down.'

Edith stands her ground. The bear nuzzles into her coat, whimpering. She recognises the other man. He's the mayor's son. He lowers his gun.

The huntsman with a feather in his hat does not. He shouts, louder this time, 'Did you hear me, girl?'

The mayor's son is staring at Edith. Then he quickly looks about him and back the way he came.

'Leave it,' he says. 'We've lost our party.'

'We've spent the morning chasing it,' says the huntsman with the feather. 'It's my kill.'

'It's not much of a bear,' says the mayor's son.

The other turns on him. 'What's wrong with you?' He moves towards Edith but the mayor's son takes hold of his jacket.

'She doesn't speak,' he says. 'Her name is Edith – she's a ghost.'

The huntsman lowers his gun.

'Edith? You mean the village girl who ran away from her wedding?'

The mayor's son nods. 'Come on,' he says, and there is panic in his voice. 'Let's find the hunting party.'

'No, wait,' says the other. 'We've caught something more significant than a bear.'

'She's a ghost.'

The huntsman with the feather waves his friend away. He's looking at Edith, eyeing her up.

'She seems to me to be made of flesh and blood,' he says. His tongue slowly wets his lips. 'And if she is a ghost, then it wouldn't matter what I did to her, would it?'

'She's cursed,' says the mayor's son. 'I'm going. Do what you want – you always do.'

Edith watches him as he runs into the forest.

The huntsman steps closer. 'Curses, like chickens, come home to roost. Don't you agree?'

The bear cub starts to wriggle and Edith lets it down onto the ground. She is aware now that something is behind her.

The huntsman looks up in disbelief at what he sees. He fumbles for his gun, his finger finds the trigger. Without a thought Edith runs at him. The gun goes off, the shot ricochets through the forest, echoes in the mountain. Crows fly from the trees, darkening the sky. The huntsman has fallen to the ground. When he looks up he sees a bear towering over Edith. She doesn't move; she shows no fear.

The huntsman finds his feet but loses his hat and turns to run but the bear lurches towards him and catches him with a swipe. His screams are lost in the bear's roar. He drops his gun and, clutching the side of his face, stumbles into the forest, his blood speckling the snow. Only then does Edith slowly turn. The bear towers above her and she bows her head as it drops to the ground and disappears into the forest, the bear cub safe on its mother's back.

It begins to snow, flake by feathery flake, until the blood is covered with a dusting of white and no one would know that the hunted and the hunters had been there. A new page is ready to be written on. Silence, thinks Edith, is like the snow: it covers secrets, makes the unacceptable acceptable. She picks up the gun and the feather from the huntsman's hat then sits on the step of the cabin listening to the snow. She hears in it a gentle sound that calms her. The snow is singing softly, the forest settling back into itself. She stays there until the heat in her is gone, grateful for her new boots and the sheepskin-lined coat, for the cabin. The primaeval forest with its murmuring pines is gathering the darkness to it and she hears the howl of a wolf. She fears there is little time left. The huntsmen will be back bringing the butcher with them. She doesn't doubt it.

Demetrius must be somewhere not far from here, she thinks. Even though his face was unseen, he was with me, I heard his voice. What a thin veil of moon and stars divides us from a different heaven that holds a thread of possibilities. Be near me again, be near me.

The hope in her is gone but still she has no desire to leave. She heard what the mayor's son called her – a ghost – but he would use another word in the village. A word that would strike at the heart of all the villagers' superstition. He would say she was one of the bloodless.

In the gloaming hour the forest looks on solemnly. Numb with cold, Edith hears again the chiming, the soft ringing of bells, just as she had on her wedding day. Holding out her hand she catches the snowflakes. Then, laughing, she opens her arms and spins round and round to the song of the snow. Tilting back her head she sees the moon rise pregnant with the night.

Giddy from spinning, she stops and in the long shadows sees him. She looks again in case her eyes have tricked her. He stands by the trees, his little dog at his heels. Edith dares not move in case a breath might mean the loss of him. Her eyes never leave his as he comes to her. She is certain she will find him made of ice and illusions. But his arms are strong about her, his eyes as blue as a winter sky, his lips warm, his kisses filled with love.

'Am I dreaming?' she asks and hears her lost voice brush his cheek.

'No, my love.'

And her voice bursts free from her and sings with the wolf into the frozen night.

\*

It's as if nothing has disturbed the peace of the cabin. The windows glow with warmth, the door stands open, inviting them to enter. She has the sensation of coming home. Demetrius closes the door, and the outside world fades away. By what clock they live concerns them not at all.

\*

Edith knows she and Demetrius spend that winter in a clearing in the forest. They never leave and they travel far by staying. He teaches her to play the violin, they make love, dance and laugh.

When he tells her about his time as a shepherd she's unsure if they aren't both there on the mountain, for she feels the warmth of the sun and sees the meadow, the flight of the swallow, the rise of the lark.

She asks if he knows who his murderer was.

'No,' he says. 'But I knew I would be killed.'

And the pang of guilt that she feels about his death rises, a serpent to bite her.

She says, quietly, 'I was to blame. If I'd never promised to marry the butcher perhaps you'd still be alive.'

'Nothing, my love, is that simple,' he says. 'I had a brother, younger than me, my parents' favourite. He wanted to take over my father's business. But in our family, the tradition is that the eldest son inherits it when his father retires.'

The light begins to fade, rooms fall and rise until all becomes still and Edith is with him in a house with a long, imposing passage. The walls are sliced in two; the lower part panelled, the upper part papered with a pattern of brooding lilies. The smell of dead flowers is noticeable. A thin young man with round glasses catches a maid and pushes her against the wall, bunching up her skirt with his other hand.

'He always was subtle in his dealings with the ladies,' says Demetrius.

'Your brother?'

'My brother.'

The light in the passage hisses and Edith doesn't know if it all happens at the same time or if she is seeing an accumulation of isolated incidents. His mother, a large, matronly woman with a well-endowed bosom, is sitting in a blood-red drawing room, surrounded by a sea of pompous furniture, heavy with the weight of inheritance. She is talking to a stiff-backed lady whose low chair puts her at a disadvantage.

'Mother is telling her friend that her daughter, Palonia, is lucky to be marrying an angel,' says Demetrius.

'Where is Palonia? And where is the angel?'

Demetrius laughs and only now does Edith notice the girl, crushed by her mother's hopes for the impending marriage. Demetrius' mother studies the girl as if to assure herself she's worthy of being sacrificed on the altar of the family name.

'The angel is my brother,' says Demetrius, 'and here's my father.'

Before them is a gentleman, imprisoned in a stiffly starched collar, walking back and forth in his study, a pendulum marking time. Behind him the walls are hung with cuckoo clocks. 'He's saying I will never amount to anything, that he sent me to university and now I intend to waste my life by becoming a shepherd.'

'Perhaps he was right,' she says.

'No – every step I took led me to you.'

'Led you to your death,' says Edith.

The cuckoo clocks all chime together.

Demetrius' perfect brother, thin as a snake, is doing up his trousers while the maid weeps.

'When my grandfather heard I was to marry you,' Demetrius says, 'he wrote to tell me to be careful – that my brother had taken up hunting.'

She is dizzy with what she's seen. 'This was your life – in that coffin of a house?' He nods. 'Why didn't your father just give the business to your brother?'

'For the same reason that you were to be married in

198

a traditional wedding dress. It has always been that way because no one had the imagination to think of another way.'

'In all my imaginings about where you'd come from, I never saw you in a house like that. I knew you were clever – lots of people are who have taught themselves about the world. But I never guessed you came from such wealth. Doesn't it make you sad to have had a family that didn't know you?'

'If I hadn't found you, I would've been wretched. The rest doesn't matter. The butcher, my brother, your father, my father. It's all the same. I was the stranger who fell in love with a magical woman and that changed everything.'

'I know nothing of the world you left.'

'That makes me love you more.'

*

In the morning – which morning? In a morning with light coming through the windows and Demetrius' arms round her, she says, 'The word "love" is too small.'

'It's a word that many claim and few find,' says Demetrius.

'May this never end,' she whispers.

He runs his finger down her neck. 'All things living and dead have a season,' he says and kisses her.

'What would we do if you were alive?' she asks.

'Much as we do now. We would worry more about money and my sheep and the roundness of your belly.'

'There will be no children.'

And then he says something that she holds tight to. 'Not this time, but there will be. This time we have winter, we have the snow.' He climbs out of bed, pulls on his trousers. 'Tonight I will play for you.'

She turns away for she can't bear to look at the wound in his back, a weeping eye that can be plainly seen.

Neither he nor his dog go hunting with her. She goes out to see what she can find for the pot. She takes the hunter's gun. There is only the one bullet, a precious gift not to be wasted on a rabbit. The knowledge of it gives her a sense of power; if anyone comes for her she at least is armed and has one chance to protect herself.

'If you catch many more birds, you might fly away on borrowed feathers,' he says.

Edith has finished the skirt and jacket she's made from her wedding dress and other pieces of fabric she found in the chest. She's embroidered them with red flowers.

Edith eats a pheasant she has trapped, cooked in plum wine and snowmelt with mushrooms and barley. He watches as he always does.

'Why weren't you wearing your boots when Misha found you?' she asks.

He thinks for a moment. 'It seems so unimportant. I was washing my feet in a stream. I saw a butterfly, and I wondered who made this world with its mountains, its valleys, and also thought to make something as delicate as the butterfly.'

'Didn't you hear the footsteps behind you?'

'Don't be sad,' he said. 'That's the difference between us.

I neither care nor have any interest in who pulled the trigger. I'm dead.' He touches her face and asks, 'Do you know what makes snow?'

'Rain,' she says.

'Rain and particles of dust. Without the dust there would be nothing for the snowflake to form itself round. Each one different, gentle, soft. The dust of me will always be there in the snow.' He looks out of the cabin window. 'The moon is full. If I play will you dance for me?'

She stands and puts on her fur hat with its antlers and feather. In the silvery pool of moonlight, she begins to move, her hands held across her chest. The music starts slowly. She is conscious of him watching her. Eyes closed, she opens her arms and whirls round and round. She takes off her jacket but the music asks for more. Layer by layer her clothes come off until she is naked apart from her hat and her boots. Only then does the dance become hers. She dances for her lover's wound, she dances for the life he didn't own, she dances for the passion that's in her. She is reborn into her skin and begins to understand this cloth of flesh pulled tight over muscle and bone and the pleasure it gives her to dance naked for herself, for her lover.

'You dance me wild,' he says as his music reaches a crescendo. Only then does the song come from deep inside her. Raw in her throat it rises until she feels the power of it against her teeth, a power older than her soul. The song is returned to her in the growl of a bear, in the howl of a wolf. Breathless she falls into his arms. And still it snows.

\*

'You are the most beautiful of women,' he says.

'Have you seen many?' Edith asks.

To her surprise, he says simply, 'Yes, but none compare to you. Now,' he says, changing the subject. 'Tell me your story. You listened to mine, it's your turn.'

'There's not much to tell.'

'I don't believe that. Try.'

She thinks she could gaze on him for all time. Then she looks down at her hands. 'I was born and brought up, and I met you.'

'His shoes were new,' he said.

'Whose shoes?'

'Whoever shot me.'

'How do you know?'

'It's the last thing I remember thinking as I lay on the ground, and he walked towards me. It's the smallness of things that matter, the brevity of a little rock can't be dismissed. It's still part of the mountain.'

\*

This night is the last. The last time she hears his music, the last time they make love. She can't tell in all their passion where he begins and she ends. They are floating over her village, they are a part of the moon and the stars.

He whispers, 'Do not fear the coming of the light.'

It isn't as if they're waking into a new day, more that they've travelled there and arrived in a different place and found the cabin to be filled with sunshine. On the table is a bunch of snowdrops.

Edith turns to him. 'It broke me once to lose you.'

'You aren't losing me. Neither will you lose your voice. I'm here. I'll always be here; my soul is with you, and you will come back to me. Dress for me. I want you to look a queen when you return to the village.'

He hands her the fur hat with its reindeer horns.

She smiles. 'I can't wear it.'

'You should,' he says. 'The more strange and wondrous you look, the more they'll respect you and leave you alone. Don't go back with your head bowed. Stand tall, be brave. The one thing men fear most is the freedom of a woman to be herself. Wild women frighten men.'

'They'll see me as a ghost or one of the bloodless.'

'They will see you and hear you, and no one will lay a hand on you.'

Demetrius hands her the violin.

'I'll look very strange dressed like this,' she says. 'Perhaps I'll be with you sooner than I think for they'll...' She stops.

He opens the cabin door. She smells the urgency of spring in the air, the snow nearly thawed, the earth bursting with life. She hears the roar of the snowmelt as it cascades into the mountain streams.

'I've left it as late as I could,' he says.

She turns from him and in that instant knows him to be gone.

*

The cabin was as derelict as it was when she first found it. She walked towards the skirted fir trees and pushed her way into the sunlight. She half expected to find she was wearing her wedding dress and was pleased that she was still in the clothes she'd made.

'This will forever be my secret,' she said aloud.

The air smelled sweet and was filled with the song of birds. Down she went to where the oak and beech grew. Far below her she saw her village, heard the church bells ringing. For a whole winter not once had she given any thought to the days of the week or the hours of the clock.

The village was pretty in the sunlight with its quaint, painted houses, the cherry trees in bloom. She walked up the cobbled street to the square and found no one about apart from the odd stray dog, a cat sleeping on a windowsill. Singing was coming from inside the church. It's Easter, she thought, and waited for the congregation to emerge.

# CHAPTER TWENTY-FIVE

## WILD WOMAN

The butcher came out of the church into the blazing spring sunshine. The moment he saw her, he stopped. He felt his heart lurch and put his hand to his chest. To everyone's surprise, he stumbled. A small thing but one that was noticed by the congregation. Una rushed to his side and he swatted her away and pointed to where Edith stood. With the sun in their eyes, it took the villagers time to make sense of what they were seeing. A wild figure in a headdress of fur, antlers and feathers stood before them, a mountain goddess descended from the summit.

'A gypsy,' pronounced the priest. He sighed. 'I thought I'd made it quite clear that the circus isn't welcome here.'

Shielding his eyes, he looked again, and it slowly dawned on him that he was staring at a dead woman. He went pale.

The doctor too squinted, then gasped in horror. 'It's not possible,' he said. 'Nobody could survive the winter on the mountain.'

The mayor said, 'My God.' And added, though no one knew what he meant by it, 'Will it ever end?'

Six elders pushed forward.

'Surely she can't be alive?' said one of them. It was a question that didn't have an answer.

Edith watched them and smiled and for the first time didn't mind being stared at. Let them look, she thought, as she turned to walk down the street and with every step she had the sensation that she was becoming taller. She put the violin under her chin and played, a Pied Piper bringing her voice back to the village. The frail and the young who hadn't attended church peered from their windows.

The cabinet maker peeped out from behind his shutters and saw a crowd following this wild creature. Fearing the worst, he hid under the stairs. It had proved a place of safety in the avalanche; perhaps it would serve again with a demon.

Only when Edith reached her house and opened the gate did she feel herself return to her normal size. With an uncharacteristic gesture, she bowed to the crowd before closing the gate behind her. And a lost memory came rushing back to greet her: the day her grandmother died, she'd blocked her ears to all that her grandmother had tried to tell her. She'd refused to listen and had run off to see Lena. When she returned, washing was still hanging in the yard and a sizeable earthenware dish was broken on the kitchen floor. Her grandmother was lying dead at the foot of the stairs.

Edith looked round the yard now. It was a wreck, and

a goat was nonchalantly munching the tops of some strag-
gly turnips. Only the walnut tree stood proud in its fresh,
spring-washed leaves. Five bedraggled hens emerged from
the henhouse. Too thin for eggs, too thin for the pan. How
could her father have let everything fall into ruin?

The house was in an even worse state, smelling of stale
wine and piss, though her bedroom was untouched. From
the middle of the kitchen, she called to the cabinet maker.

'Where are you?'

It was strange, even to her, to hear her own voice in the
house again.

A pathetic whimpering came from under the stairs and
she opened the cupboard. He was thin like the hens, his eyes
sunk into their sockets.

'I'm not a well man,' he said. 'Are you a demon? Have
you come to take me to hell? It was an accident – I didn't
touch her – she lost her footing.'

For a moment Edith couldn't think what the old fool was
blabbering about. He crawled out of the cupboard. Still on
his knees, he said, 'Just give me another chance.'

She hadn't imagined that her appearance would have such
a dramatic effect. Demetrius had been right.

The cabinet maker seemed to be in a mood to talk and
Edith decided to say nothing.

'You see, I had to do something. The old woman was going
to take Edith away. I couldn't let her – she was my daughter,
my property, not hers. You're not Edith. You look like her but
you're a demon. Please, demon, it was an accident.'

The cabinet maker jumped when Edith spoke.

'No, it was no accident. Even then, you'd already made your deal with the butcher that I should be bride meat.'

'I gave that woman a roof over her head, food, a place to stay. I indulged her by letting Edith call her Grandmother.'

'Without her and her stories, we would have been penniless. I go away for the winter and look at you, you lazy drunk. I'm not going to stay long but while I'm here this place will be clean and tidy. And you will clean and tidy it.'

He scratched his head, trying to make something work in his wine-soaked brain. Finally, he said, 'What kind of demon are you?'

'An angry one. And I am Edith.'

'No,' he said backing away. 'She's dead. But I grant you, demon, she isn't buried because her remains haven't been found. You are one of the bloodless. Edith doesn't talk.'

She stared at him. 'You will clean the house,' she said, and her father scurried away to fetch the broom and a pail.

By sunset, he had swept the floors, washed the windows and scrubbed the table. Never once had Edith taken her eyes off him or lifted a hand to help.

'I need a drink,' said the cabinet maker.

Edith stood and blocked the door. 'No,' she said. 'You're not going out tonight to beg for alcohol.'

'I can't do without a drink, I can't,' he said.

'I know that,' said Edith. She went into her room and lifted the two floorboards under which she had kept a small supply of lentils, barley and oats, and five bottles of plum brandy. She had always been fearful that one day there might be nothing in the store cupboard.

She put one bottle on the table with two glasses. For the first time that afternoon, the cabinet maker's eyes lit up.

'You've never been grateful for anything, have you?' she said.

Her father's hands shook as the glass found his lips. He looked up at her and said, 'I'm grateful for the plum brandy.'

\*

The butcher called a meeting of the elders and told them that they must agree to ban anyone from going near the cabinet maker's daughter. For all his bombast there was a sense of unease among the elders, as if something more than snow had melted.

'Remember what happened to the bear hunters?' the butcher said.

How could they forget? The mayor's son had sworn he'd witnessed Edith tear the flesh from his friend's face and suck the blood from him. Nor had they forgotten that the mayor's son had told them how he and his friend had got away: the sun had shone through the trees into Edith's eyes and she, being terrified of sunlight, had disappeared into the snow.

Today they'd seen her, as solid as a Sunday prayer. Wild-looking, yes, but she did not shun the sunlight. The six elders had noted that the butcher had stumbled when he saw her and clutched at his heart. Now, as he bible-thumped his warning, they saw a man irrationally obsessed with the woman he'd lost.

'The two young men were brought back to the village,' said the butcher, warming once more to his favourite subject, 'and you know what the huntsman said as he lay dying.'

They did. Seven bears. Edith stood tall among seven bears. Her feet never touching the ground. It had sounded suspiciously like a fairy tale Edith's grandmother used to tell, of the seven bears and the brier rose. Wasn't there also a princess in the story whose feet never touched the ground? They also knew that the doctor had insisted that the huntsman's wounds were consistent with those of a bear attack.

'The mayor's son has been ill ever since, a sickness brought on by Edith,' said the butcher. 'We should arrest her, question her, before she infects us all.'

'Infects us? With what?' asked the miller.

'Bewitches us. Remember the wedding dress, the avalanche? We must question her about the attack on the huntsman.'

That Easter Sunday, the six elders who all that winter had felt themselves to be a nodding chorus to the butcher's demands, saw a chink of light. Easter was, after all, a time of resurrection, of new beginnings.

'On another matter,' said an elder, 'an important matter, we want to know who gave you permission to release the shepherd's body to his brother. The mayor didn't sign those papers.'

'This,' he said, hitting his fist into his hand, 'this matter of the attack is more important than a dead shepherd.'

The other six elders strongly disagreed.

\*

The mayor's wife, Georgeta, hadn't been among the congregation that morning. Her son had had a bad night.

At their midday meal her husband told her about the creature who'd appeared outside the church.

'Rubbish!' she said, shooting a furious look at him. 'I refuse to believe that Edith is one of the bloodless.'

'How else could she have survived such a harsh winter?' said the mayor.

'By her own wit,' said his wife.

'You still doubt our son?' said the mayor.

'Something terrible happened in the forest. He may or he may not have witnessed his friend being attacked by a bear. He may or may not have seen Edith. As for the rest, no, I don't believe a word. At the heart of his illness isn't Edith or magical powers but the fact that he lied. And that lie is what is making him ill.'

'She was wearing a hat of fur and feathers,' said the mayor. 'She wasn't of this world.'

'Poppycock,' said Georgeta and she reached for another potato.

\*

The cobbler had insisted that Vanda stayed at home that Easter Sunday morning. He didn't want his wife upset by her father, not now she was expecting their child. And Una was refusing to have anything to do with her.

'A baby?' she'd said when Vanda told her she was pregnant. 'At your age? I would have thought you were past all that.'

'I don't believe it,' said Vanda when the cobbler told her Edith's ghost had returned to the village. 'I'll go and see her.'

'I'm not sure…' said the cobbler.

'Hasn't it occurred to you that my father won't want anyone to see Edith because she got the better of him, and might do so again? If I know him, he will be plotting some way to harm her, just as he's harmed Misha and the cabinet maker.'

He looked up at Vanda as she stood then bent to kiss him. The newness of their relationship made him feel young again. He had been stepfather to Misha, but this was his own child, born out of love, not hate. And they were still young, perhaps there would be more.

'You're right,' said the cobbler.

It was Misha who was the first to see Edith.

# CHAPTER TWENTY-SIX

## THE HOPE BOX

There was a knock on the door and fearing another demon – or worse still, the butcher – the cabinet maker tightened his grip on the plum brandy.

'If you're a demon, go away,' he said and screwed up his face, dreading the sound of the butcher's voice.

But it was Misha who said, 'Can I come in?' Still clutching the bottle, the cabinet maker nervously opened the door. 'Where's Edith?' asked Misha.

'Dead,' said the cabinet maker. 'But there's a demon who looks like her – in there.' He pointed to Edith's bedroom. 'A demon,' he whispered, 'who can conjure up plum brandy.' He gazed at Misha's bulging pockets with interest. 'What have you there? Wine?'

'Yes, and bread and cheese,' said Misha and put them on the table.

The cabinet maker looked round and was shocked to see his daughter.

'Edith! What have you done with the demon?' he asked her.

'The demon told me that as you've been obedient, I can stay here. But if you return to your old ways, the demon will be back to collect you.'

'Me? Are you sure? Me?'

'You,' said Edith.

The cabinet maker looked from the plum brandy in his hand to the wine on the table. 'One glass from that bottle before bed?'

'No,' said Edith.

The cabinet maker scurried away to his room. She and Misha heard him drag a chair across the floor to bar the door. 'No demon can get me now,' he muttered.

Edith said, 'His mind is going.'

'There's nothing dead about you,' said Misha. 'Or demon-like.'

'You didn't see my hat.'

'I did. And I heard you play the violin.'

'I thought my father would have sold all the clothes from my hope box but he hadn't, so I was able to change.'

'He missed you,' said Misha.

'No.'

'He did. The butcher treated him badly all winter. He took back everything he'd given him before the wedding – the logs, the food, the wine. He instructed everyone in the village not to lift a hand to help him. The priest preached a sermon about him, about the sickness of excessive drinking and the evil of a father who can't control his offspring.'

Edith suddenly saw Misha had been bringing food and firewood for her father and knew it was he who had brought her the gifts of rabbits and birds when she'd first found the cabin.

'You brought him food?' Misha nodded. 'Thank you.'

'I couldn't do any more for him. I wanted to but whenever I came here some neighbour or other would report me to the elders.'

Edith put out the bread and cheese.

'Your voice is deeper than I remember,' he said.

'And you look sad,' said Edith. 'How's Lena?'

'I don't know. I've hardly seen her since the day you ran away. The butcher turned Lena's mother against me. He looked after her and her daughter and in return Lena is forbidden to see me. Our baby will be born soon and I want to be a good father but the butcher told the widow not to waste her daughter on the village idiot.'

'What does Lena think?'

Misha shrugged. 'She's almost a prisoner so I don't know what Lena believes. I don't know if she thinks of me at all.'

Edith cut the bread.

'An avalanche,' said Misha, 'the village is isolated and the butcher becomes all-powerful. But he had no power over you. You are a festering wound to his pride – even more so now you've come back from the dead.'

Edith poured Misha a glass of wine. 'Is Demetrius buried in the churchyard?' she asked.

'What do you think?'

'I think his family took him back to the town.'

'As soon as the road was open – about two weeks ago. His brother and an undertaker came to collect the body. After they'd gone the butcher didn't hesitate to tell everyone that the matter was closed. There would be no investigation. I'm sorry.'

'You have nothing to be sorry about.'

'I do. I should have told you something, and I didn't. I said to myself that when I had the answer, I would.'

Edith said nothing. She imagined she was holding a bowl into which secrets could be safely poured without fear of anyone hearing them again.

Staring at his hands, Misha told her of the evening he'd met Demetrius on the mountain and about the letter, the unread words that had been weights on his heart.

'I think he knew he was going to be killed. Just before dawn broke he recited a poem, the words to a melody he'd been playing.'

*Full moon, high sea,*
*Great man thou shall be.*
*Redding dawn, cloudy sky,*
*Bloody death shalt thou die.*

'We'd spoken of many things that night, and he'd told me that words can chain us. I asked what he meant and he said I had let my grandfather's word for me define me as a simpleton. He said, "You know it's not true and you mustn't let that word haunt your life."'

Edith knew this about listening: that it became harder to hold the bowl. It would be easier to put it down, to question, to comfort. But instead she let the silence gather him in.

'That's not what I meant to say. I wanted to tell you about Demetrius' brother. The following morning when I left with the letter, I met a huntsman coming up the mountain. He asked where the shepherd was. I saw Demetrius' brother when he came to collect the body. He was wearing glasses but with or without glasses I knew it was the huntsman I'd met on the mountain.' He looked at Edith and said, 'You know all this, don't you?'

'Demetrius told me his brother had taken up hunting,' said Edith. 'And I know the butcher was hired to guide the hunting party.'

'He was on the mountain that morning too – it was then he took the letter from me,' said Misha. 'As for the rest, I have my suspicions – my grandfather would have been on hand if...'

He paused for a moment. 'I think you are a shaman,' he said, 'a magical woman who can save us. It's been a hard winter and your father and I are not the only ones the butcher has made life hell for. The butcher has become...'

'...a monster?' said Edith. 'He always was.'

They sat for a while in silence before Misha asked, 'What are you going to do?'

Edith stared out of the window. Above the roof of the henhouse the night sky was clear, freckled with a fistful of stars.

'I'm going to write down some of my grandmother's stories and one of my own. And, once you and Lena are married, I'll be gone.'

Misha laughed. 'If,' he said.

'There are no ifs. Tell me about your mother.'

'She's pregnant.'

'No!'

'Yes – and she's happy, she even laughs. The cobbler looks younger. At first, I thought any day she would wake up, and the enchantment would be broken. Even my stepfather thought that.'

'Stepfather?' said Edith.

'You know the truth,' said Misha.

'I do, but I wasn't sure you did.'

'I had time on the mountain to think. Mountains do that. They were here long before man, long before we had the weapon of words. The butcher has cast doubt on Mother, told everyone that she's not well in the head.'

'No one can believe that,' said Edith.

'No one can afford not to believe everything he says. We've been isolated all winter and the butcher made sure that if anyone needed anything only he could supply it. So now they're all even more indebted to the butcher.'

'What of Sorina?' asked Edith.

'She's lived at the butcher's since you ran off. He insisted he needed someone to keep house for him. Una dragged her there, Sorina begging her mother not to make her go but Una was hearing none of it. Half the village witnessed the scene. Sorina looks older than her years. I tried to tell Una whose child I am but she wouldn't listen.' He finished his wine. 'I should go – it's late.'

'Thank you,' said Edith.

'For what? For not bringing you the letter?'

'For being a good and brave friend.'

Misha stood up to leave. 'Lock your door and be careful, Edith,' he said.

*

'Misha told me you'd found your voice,' said Flora when she came the next morning with a pot of honey. 'And we have lots to talk about. How on earth did you survive all winter?' But it became apparent that Edith didn't want to talk about it and Flora changed the subject.

'The butcher called a meeting of the elders yesterday,' she said. 'I heard this morning that he wants you arrested.'

'For what?' asked Edith. 'Not wanting to marry him?'

'The mayor's son claimed he saw you attack his friend.'

'Do you think I'm capable of that?'

'Of course I don't.'

'Why is the mayor's son lying?' said Edith. 'He ran off when his friend was considering attacking me. Did the rest of the hunting party bring them back to the village?'

'Not straight away. The two young men were lost for a while. The butcher found them. I wouldn't be at all surprised if he convinced them they'd been attacked by you. The mayor's son has been unwell ever since.'

'Misha told me that once Demetrius' brother had collected the body, the butcher announced it was the end of the matter.'

'It isn't,' said Flora. 'My brother had a letter from Demetrius' father, thanking him for preserving his son's body so well. He wrote that there will be an investigation. He sent money, too, payment for my brother. And this for you.'

Edith opened the envelope. It contained money and a photograph taken of Demetrius when he graduated from university.

'He was very handsome,' said Flora.

Edith closed her eyes to stop the tears. Still they escaped. When his father finds out the truth, she thought, what will be left of the family? How will his father ever recover, knowing what his youngest son has done?

She walked with Flora to the gate and after her friend left, she gazed at the sky. In the song of the birds she heard Demetrius' melodies, in the wind she felt the touch of his hand, in the warmth of the sun, his embrace.

\*

No one else came to the cabinet maker's house, not Vanda, Georgeta or Lena. Edith knew she was viewed with suspicion and her movements were reported to the butcher. Everywhere she went she was stared at and neighbours whispered behind her back. She realised she had become a stranger among them.

Edith took some of the money from the envelope to buy much-needed supplies but both the grocer and the baker refused to serve her.

'If my father has run up debt,' she said, 'I will settle the bill.'

It angered her to discover that her father owed them nothing; that the shop keepers would rather have seen him starve to death than disobey the butcher. It was a tragedy that one man could have enslaved the small community with his cruelty.

*

The cabinet maker was mending the henhouse, singing to himself. Edith was clearing out the cupboard under the stairs when her father abruptly stopped singing. She became aware of someone standing behind her.

'I like nothing better than a woman on her knees,' he said.

Edith pushed the hair out of her eyes and stood up to face the butcher.

# CHAPTER TWENTY-SEVEN

## HIS MOTHER'S SHAWL

'No one makes a fool of me,' said the butcher. 'Do you think you can just walk back into this village dressed like a vagabond? Where did you go? You couldn't survive on the mountain in the winter we've just had. So tell me – unless you've lost your tongue again – where did you go? Do you know what I think? I think you ran away to join the gypsies…' he moved close to her and hissed '…like the whore you are.'

Sure he had the better of her, he waited for her reply. Edith stared at him, unblinking. He looked anywhere and everywhere but at her.

'I was only small when I saw your mother in our walnut tree,' said Edith. Her self-assured voice hit the butcher as hard as if she'd struck him.

'Have you lost your mind like your father?' he said. 'What are you talking about?'

'Your mother was wearing an embroidered shawl in

purples and golds. I remember thinking that they were ugly colours in an ugly pattern. She told me that she'd been taken by the filth man and that she was waiting for her son at the crossroads to take him to hell where he belonged. She said more besides but I didn't understand. I asked my grandmother what I should do. I had to tell your mother to leave me alone. I was too young to be told of your crimes. Your mother left, and I didn't see her again. I once asked my grandmother if she had ever seen one of the bloodless. She said no, but that I had – your mother. I see her now too. She stands to your right, she breathes in your ear.'

The butcher's eyes narrowed with rage. 'How dare you speak my mother's name.'

'I never knew her name,' said Edith, 'but I knew she was your mother. I'm not afraid of you and I'm not afraid of death. If you kill me it matters little. But my advice is leave my father and me alone. You've got away with your part in Demetrius' murder but it will be different if you lay a hand on my father or me. I know what you did, butcher. I know you.'

'Father?' Una was standing in the doorway.

The world came rushing back to the butcher and for a moment he wasn't sure what he'd heard or where he was. His hands curled into fists, his knuckles white. An uncontrollable furnace of rage burned inside him at this creature, this woman who had the audacity to speak to him in such a manner about his mother.

Una, on her way to her father's house, had heard his anger

and seen the cabinet maker, motionless by the henhouse. From the verandah she'd listened to Edith's calm voice and hadn't dared move until that moment.

The butcher looked at her as if he didn't recognise his own daughter. He pushed his lips together. 'Ugly like your sister,' he said. 'Both of you, ugly. But at least you're on my side.'

'Father,' said Una again.

'What are you doing here?'

'You asked me to come to your house,' she said.

Only now did he realise he'd spoken the last words aloud. He pushed past Una into the yard.

'What are you trying to do?' she said to Edith. 'Put another curse on my father? You bewitched him once, but you'll not do it again. I won't allow it.'

She turned and joined her father.

Edith watched them from the verandah and wondered how long Una had been there and how much she'd heard. By her pallor, Edith thought, time enough to have heard what she'd said.

At the gate the butcher stopped dead and only then did Una look at him and see he was still filled with fury. She went back to Edith.

'My father did you the honour of asking you to be his bride,' she said. 'He offered to take you out of this pigsty, to live a life with… with…' She waved her arms, searching her mind for the ultimate prize. 'To live a life with a goose-feather eiderdown.'

The foolishness of what she was saying made Edith laugh. Una slapped her face.

'Enough,' shouted the butcher. Feeling himself vindicated, he marched back and took hold of Una's arm.

The cabinet maker, who'd heard every word and was still frozen to the spot outside the henhouse, found his voice.

'At least,' he said, 'we live in distinguished poverty.'

The second he'd spoken he regretted it for the butcher strode towards him. Edith, quick on her feet, ran and stood between them. The butcher spat on the ground, a gobbet of saliva narrowly missing her skirt.

'Not a thing, not one thing will you be allowed in this village. No shop will sell to you, no one will give you wine, and anyone who does will be punished by me.'

'And who made you a little king?' said Edith.

The butcher stared at her white neck, her beautiful, unblemished skin, her defiant eyes, her extraordinary white hair. 'Kill her,' his mother whispered. 'Kill her.' His hand was drawn instinctively to Edith's neck, he felt the pulse of life beat in her and, with one hand, he pressed. She didn't resist. Butter couldn't have been softer. She smiled at him. Una's scream brought him back into the moment, breaking through his searing rage. He felt the blood pounding in his head and he let go. Edith crumpled to the floor.

'Oh – Father!' said Una. 'Oh God.'

Outside the gate a small group had gathered. The butcher dragged Una through the onlookers.

'It's your fault,' he said, 'you interfering bitch.'

The cabinet maker was on his knees, begging the demon to bring Edith back to life when Misha ran into the yard.

*

Edith is in a sunlit forest, amid a mosaic of bluebells and primroses. The trees, hungry for the light, reach for the dazzling blue sky. She hears Demetrius' voice. *'It's not winter, Edith. Turn back. Choose to live.'*

*

She woke, gasping for breath. She was in bed.

'Help me sit her up,' said Vanda to her son.

'Is she alive?' asked the cabinet maker, wiping his nose on his sleeve.

'Yes,' said Vanda. 'Misha saved her. Bring some water. And some brandy.'

'There's no brandy,' said the cabinet maker. 'With Edith's permission, the demon brings me one bottle every night as long as I'm good.'

'Take the old man to our house,' said Vanda to Misha, 'and bring back the brandy.'

When they'd gone, she said, 'I thank the Lord you're alive. Whatever did you say to him? No, it doesn't matter. I should have come sooner, but my husband…' Edith took Vanda's hand and squeezed it. 'You haven't lost your voice again?'

Edith coughed then said, 'No. It's a little croaky, that's all.'

Vanda brushed her hair from her face. Edith slept and dreamed of Demetrius.

*

The butcher had left Una in the middle of the street, telling her to go home. In his house, he closed the door and pulled the parlour shutters to so that the room was dark. He poured himself a drink. He shouldn't have done that. It was a mistake, but the girl had enraged him. How dare she look at him as if he were dirt. How dare she not apologise. 'Sorry. Sorry, I humiliated you.' Just one sorry would have sufficed.

'It was a mistake, Mother,' he said. 'A mistake. And worse still, Una saw it.'

In the gloom of the room, his mother was sitting in her favourite chair.

'You should have had your moment with Edith alone,' she said.

'Go away.'

'You would be nothing without me.'

He threw his glass at the apparition.

Sorina opened the door. 'Did you call for me, Grandpa?'

'Yes,' said the butcher. 'Go and fetch my mother's shawl.'

# CHAPTER TWENTY-EIGHT

## KNOWLEDGE FORGOTTEN

By the time the sun set that day Misha had moved into the cabinet maker's house. Vanda had insisted. It was for Edith's safety, she said, and no matter how much Edith protested, Vanda was adamant.

Edith had a feeling that Misha might have another motive. Her old bedroom in the attic looked directly onto Lena's mother's house. When they were young, and Lena's father still alive, he'd put up a pulley system from Lena's window to hers so they could pass messages to each other. She'd forgotten about it until she was showing Misha where he was to sleep.

'It's dusty,' she said, looking around the small room. The gaps between the floorboards were so wide that you could see the kitchen below and hear every word spoken there. She wondered if her father had sat on the bed and listened to her grandmother telling her that the two of them were going to leave the village. There it was, glinting in the deep pool of her memory – knowledge forgotten.

'Edith?' said Misha.

'Sorry,' said Edith, 'I was remembering something.'

'Can I see if I can make the pulley work?' said Misha.

\*

The afternoon became evening and the oxcarts trundled over the cobblestones into the village, a drumbeat for a sunset. The farmers returned from the fields while the women stood gossiping on their doorsteps. They stopped when they saw the priest.

'Good evening,' he said, raising his hat to them.

He knew they'd been talking about the butcher's attack on Edith. He was on his way to have a word with him.

In his slaughterhouse, his hand resting on his favourite knife, the butcher felt calmness return to him, his pent-up rage spent. He breathed in the cold evening air as the day was lost in darkness. It wouldn't surprise him if there was late snow. He picked up his knife and returned to the parlour where his mother still waited in the shadows near the cuckoo clock.

He was pouring himself a drink when he heard the double knock on the front door. The butcher opened it without bothering to see who it was; only the priest knocked that way. He turned from him and went into the parlour.

'What were you thinking?' said the priest.

'A drink?' said the butcher.

'No, thank you.'

'Can you see her?' said the butcher.

For a moment the priest thought he meant Edith. 'You could have killed her. What you did this afternoon was witnessed by half the village. They're out there now, whispering about it.'

'She's sitting where she always sits.'

The priest was tripped up by an altogether more worrying thought – the butcher was becoming unhinged.

'Who?' he asked nervously.

'My mother,' said the butcher. He sat down heavily and pointed into the dark of the room. 'She's there.'

The priest had worked with the butcher long enough and profitably enough to know to handle him with care when certain moods were on him.

'How did she survive?' said the butcher, his eyes fixed on the apparition. 'No one can survive a winter on the mountain.'

'Your mother?' said the priest.

'No – Edith!' shouted the butcher.

The priest took a step back when light caught the silver blade of the knife the butcher was playing with. The room felt uncomfortably hot.

'You must pull yourself together,' said the priest gently, using the voice he saved for the confessional, for gathering little items of gossip. Some with hooks enough to bring in a tidy sum. 'We have so much at stake.'

'Even you are scared of me,' said the butcher. 'Look at you. A frightened mouse. Edith isn't scared. She's the only one who's ever stood up to me.' He got up and moved close to the priest. 'That soft neck – I dreamed of strangling her – she was mine by rights. I've never had a beautiful woman. They've all been pig ugly – even Sorina looks ugly when she weeps. She always weeps. Go, Priest. Get out of here before I cut off your tail.'

\*

Night, and all was dark apart from an occasional light in a window; the closing of shutters the only sound as the silence of the mountain settled over the village.

Misha helped Edith cook supper. The minute the meal was over the cabinet maker put on his hat and asked if he could go to the inn.

'No,' said Edith, bringing a near-empty bottle of plum brandy for him.

The cabinet maker sighed and took the bottle to his room, barricading the door as he did every night. Neither Misha nor Edith heard him put a chair under his window and climb out.

Misha had brought a bottle of schnapps. Edith poured them both a glass and said, 'My grandmother would gather all the gossip, all the fears of the village, add her own ingredients and make a soup of words. She would tell a tale that felt as if it was yours alone. The room would go dark and it seemed to me that the story became a ball of light for you to catch.'

'They're powerful when you tell them aloud,' Misha said. 'Would they be as strong if they were written?'

'That's a good question.'

She took out the violin and put it under her chin. In the flicker of the candle flame Misha could see an audience would be enthralled by her music, by her beauty, just as they would be by her grandmother's stories.

Edith put the bow to the strings and played a melody that floated out of the window and was heard in the stillness of the night by many villagers on the edge of sleep.

After Misha had gone to bed Edith went to her room and closed the door. She sat on the floor and looked again at the circus scenes painted on her hope box and thought about Misha's question. Her grandmother's stories had a wildness at their heart, they glimmered with the possibilities of freedom, of another life, a life unlived. Misha was right – they weren't meant to be written down. Could one snowflake tell the whole story of snow when each was individually made round a grain of dust? The same was true, she thought, of her grandmother's stories. She'd told them round grains of truth and each became something different. If Edith was to write them down, all the snowflakes would be the same. They would lose their energy, lose the power to free a girl from a cage. Words, like the music of the violin, needed to be heard and she had voice enough for that.

I will be the storyteller and my stories will be the light. They will be told again by others and not even death will blow out the candle or silence the words. She had her grandmother's coat of fables; she had her fur hat with the antler horns; she was no longer shy, no longer silent. And with that thought, she climbed into bed and drifted off into dreams.

\*

The moon was lost behind a cloud as soft, late snow dusted the houses. The innkeeper collected the last of the glasses, lifted the cabinet maker to his feet and opened the door. For a moment a beer spill of golden light shone onto the cobbles.

Stumbling into the darkness the cabinet maker shouted, 'Good night.'

He paused for a piss, wetting himself in the process. 'Never mind,' he said as the inn's light went out, and he felt as he always did, abandoned by his one true love, the bottle. Wrapped in melancholy he comforted himself with the thought that he would be back at the inn tomorrow. And for no reason that he could think of, the tale of the heartbeats came to him. The darkness that had been above him now seemed to smother him. It flickered with snowflakes and tiny blue fishes swam before his eyes as he blindly meandered towards his bed. A stray dog passed him in the street.

'Good night, dear respected creature,' he said, and as the ground lost its solidity he felt an arm take hold of his. 'Thank you, demon, my legs aren't behaving themselves. We won't tell Edith,' he whispered.

\*

Misha sat on the bed. He'd put an oil lamp near the open window and carefully pegged his letter to the cord. Now, with a judder, it made its butterfly way towards Lena's window. To Misha's relief she opened the shutter and smiled at him. He pointed to the letter. That night for the first time he felt there was hope.

\*

Una's house was bigger than her sister's and she had a bigger bed with a goose-feather eiderdown. Her husband was more prosperous than Vanda's. She regretted that she and Vanda didn't speak these days. A flint of jealousy struck a flame in her. To think that Vanda's husband still… still… and now a baby. Una's husband hardly ever touched her.

This year, she hoped, Sorina would be married. Una had her eye on the mayor's son as a potential husband for her. She firmly believed girls shouldn't choose their husbands; it should be left to the elders of the village, wise men like her father. Of course, she'd mentioned the mayor's son to him. But it wasn't a match for her daughter that kept her awake. No, what gnawed at her was what she'd heard pass between her father and Edith; what Edith had said about Grandma's shawl. Una shuddered at the memory of the old woman with her mean eyes and hard hands. She'd remained frightened of the shawl long after Grandma had died. But why?

*

Una woke in the dawn of a cold spring day. Her husband rolled away from her. She sat up and tried to rid herself of a nightmare. She was in her father's house and she couldn't find Vanda. It's hard to know your age in dreams, she thought. There was a sound coming from her father's bedroom. She pushed open the door, and there was Vanda, the shawl round her shoulders, blood on her nightdress.

It was only a nightmare, Una said to herself as she dressed. But by the time she was lighting the stove, the dream had transported itself into a memory, held in place by time. She must have been twelve. The memory became sharper, and the harder she pushed at its blade, the deeper it cut. She gazed out at the yard with its light dusting of snow and knew with absolute clarity who she'd last seen wearing Grandma's shawl: her daughter Sorina.

One small crack appeared in the walls of righteousness that she had meticulously built over the years, lie upon lie until the past became acceptable. Now the walls crumbled to dust. Why hadn't she listened to her sister, to Misha? They had both tried to warn her, to protect her, and she had given her daughter to that monster. She rocked back and forth as one memory overlaid another.

I did that. Pig stupid. I did that. Pig ugly. And the tears that threatened to demolish her suddenly froze. She saw exactly what she was going to do.

Later, she remembered everything except the walk to her

father's house. No one was awake. She'd gone straight to the cupboard where he kept his hunting gun and the bullets. She had loaded the gun the way he had taught her. A memory itched her mind. She was a child, she'd asked the butcher if he loved her.

'You and your sister – both of you are disappointments,' he'd said. 'Your mother didn't even have the strength to give me a son.'

He never answered my question, she thought. The butcher's bedroom was on the ground floor. She'd opened the bedroom door just as she had in her dream.

Now she stood at the foot of her father's bed.

'What do you want?' said the butcher, waking. He saw the gun and sat up with a start. 'Put it down, Una.'

For once, she didn't do what her father told her. She pointed the gun at his chest and pulled the trigger.

# CHAPTER TWENTY-NINE

## THE BEST CHINA

The second Sorina heard the gunshot, she was wide awake, every part of her alert, her heart pounding.

She went silently down the stairs and stopped in the hall. She could see the outline of her mother, framed in the doorway of the butcher's bedroom.

'Mother?' Sorina said into the darkness.

Una didn't turn to her. 'I've killed you,' she said as if to herself. Sorina crept closer. 'I meant to hit your chest.'

'Mother,' said Sorina again.

Still Una didn't appear to know she was there. 'The gun threw me back.'

Now Sorina could see beyond her to where the butcher sat bolt upright in bed, the top of his head blown off, a halo of red splattered on the bedroom wall.

Sorina stared in wonder at the sight. Was he really dead? She felt her whole being fill with excitement. He was dead.

'The shawl,' said Una, and Sorina jumped. 'I saw you

wearing that terrible shawl. I should have known – I should have killed him then.'

'Come away, Mother.'

'Is he dead?'

'Yes, Mother.'

Sorina couldn't take her eyes off the gruesome sight. The butcher's eyes were wide open, his mouth too, his face a carnival mask.

'Good,' said Una. 'That's good.'

Sorina tried to coax her mother into the kitchen.

'No. I must stay here in case he comes back, one of the bloodless like his mother.'

That thought frightened Sorina. She had often heard the butcher talking to his mother. Sorina had to think. She wished her mind wasn't so slow. She was so used to taking orders from the butcher that now she had no will of her own.

Then the image of Edith in her fur hat with the antlers came to her. Yes, she thought, the only person in the whole village to have disobeyed the butcher. The wild woman would know what to do.

Sorina left her mother talking to the dead man and walked as fast as she dared for she didn't want to draw attention to herself.

Look as if you are fetching an egg, not as if your mother has shot your grandfather. The sun had come out and melted the snow. It's going to be a fine day, she thought. I must remember to water the plants.

She looked up to see Edith and Misha coming towards her.

'Sorina…' Edith said.

'How did you know?'

\*

Misha and Lena had spent all night sending messages to each other. In the early dawn Misha had seen the unmistakable figure of Una walking determinedly towards the butcher's. He'd heard the gunshot and run downstairs to find Edith fully dressed, staring at the walnut tree in the yard.

'Something's happened,' she'd said.

\*

Inside the gloom of the butcher's house, Edith said, 'Light the stove and open all the windows.'

Sorina was grateful to be told what to do and disappeared into the parlour. The light from its window suddenly illuminated the dark hall that led to the butcher's bedroom. Una was still there, still holding the hunting gun.

'I had to shoot him,' she said when she saw Misha and Edith.

Edith looked into the room and felt vomit rise in her throat. Oh God, she thought. Either Una or I will hang for this. She took the weapon from Una and laid it on the floor at the side of the bed.

'You were the only one to stand up to him,' said Una. 'I didn't. Why didn't I?'

Edith led her to the kitchen and sat her in a chair.

Sorina said, 'What shall I do now?'

What shall I do now, thought Edith. How do I find a way out of this?

'Put the kettle on the stove,' she said, 'and bring the teapot and some cups.'

Sorina slowly put out the cups, the best china that was reserved for weddings, births and funerals.

'Now sit down and we'll have some tea,' said Edith.

She looked at the girl, a child really. Just a child. And she remembered the sisters arguing, Vanda's words, the unspoken meaning between them. She thought of what the butcher had done when Vanda was the same age as Sorina, of Vanda's pregnancy. The story became as clear to Edith as if someone had told it to her.

Sorina felt Edith's gaze and looked up at her. Edith saw trust in her eyes and nodded. Yes, there was a way.

'Shall I pour the tea?' said Sorina.

'Turn the pot three times,' said her mother, 'otherwise it's unlucky. Three times and the devil won't stay here.'

'I'll get the doctor and the mayor,' said Misha. 'Don't let anyone else in.'

It felt like an age before he returned with the doctor and behind them, the priest.

'We met the priest in the street – he insisted on coming.'

He led the men to the bedroom.

Edith, Una and Sorina waited in silence. They heard the scrape of a chair and the doctor coughing. He and the priest were talking as they came into the kitchen.

'Who did this? Was it you?' said the priest, pointing at Edith. 'Just as I thought – you.'

'It was suicide,' said Edith.

'I don't believe it was,' said the doctor. 'It's difficult to shoot oneself in the head with a hunting gun.'

'And the butcher was a God-fearing man – he would never do such a thing,' said the priest.

They were joined by the mayor. 'There's quite a crowd outside,' he said and looked round the kitchen. 'I hear the butcher has been shot dead. What happened?'

Edith noticed the mayor seemed remarkably cheerful.

'The butcher has been murdered by this woman...' he pointed at Edith.

'No,' said Una. 'I shot him.' The priest, the doctor and the mayor stared at her. 'I did it. That word – you just said it. Yes, murder. I murdered him.'

'Mother,' said Sorina, 'don't say that.'

'Better lock her up,' said the priest to the mayor. 'She's confessed to the murder.'

'Don't be too hasty, Priest,' said Edith. 'Nothing is that simple.'

The priest was horrified to be spoken to in such a manner by a woman.

'It's what the law demands – justice,' he said.

'Justice,' said Edith, repeating the word as if to see how it tasted. 'Justice. Yes, that is what's wanted here.'

'Out,' the priest shouted. 'You two women, out now. Una stays. Misha, fetch the elders.'

'No,' said Misha.

'I agree,' said Edith. 'I wouldn't do that.'

'You have the audacity to tell me what we should do?'

'Doctor,' said Edith. 'How many times did Sorina come to you? With, of course, her grandfather's permission.'

She had seen how Sorina had sunk into her chair when the priest spoke and she was certain that her instinct was correct.

'Don't answer that,' said the priest. 'No woman should question our judgement.'

And Edith knew she was right.

'Well, Mayor?' continued the priest. 'Don't you agree? This is a matter for the elders.'

The mayor poured himself a cup of tea, added honey and stirred it with a small teaspoon. A lightness of heart had engulfed him when he'd heard of the butcher's death. 'I couldn't imagine the butcher owning such delicate spoons,' he said.

'He didn't,' said Una. 'They were part of my mother's dowry.'

'Doctor, perhaps you would answer the question,' said the mayor.

'This is preposterous,' said the priest.

'Twice,' said the doctor. 'I had no choice.'

'And each time it was for what reason?' asked Edith.

'None of your business,' said the priest.

Sorina reached for Edith's hand. She sat up straight and said, 'The doctor got rid of two babies. The first baby was made at the hunting party last year. The second was a month ago.'

'Whose baby was that?' asked Edith.

'Grandpa's.'

'Is that true, Doctor?' said the mayor.

'Yes,' said the doctor. 'The priest sent her to me.'

'Did you, Priest?' asked the mayor.

'I'm not going to be bullied into an answer. This girl,' said the priest, pointing at Sorina, 'is a liar and a whore.'

Una had shown no signs of emotion at the shocking revelations. She had sat quietly drinking her tea but the priest's words brought her back to herself. She stood up and slapped the priest round the face – once – twice. Misha pulled her away and she let out a howl.

'I'm so sorry, Mother,' said Sorina.

Una knelt by her daughter and put her arms round her. 'I'm the one who should be sorry,' she said.

'I'm leaving,' said the priest. 'Neither of you are man enough to stand up to these women.'

'No,' said Edith as Misha blocked the door. 'You're going nowhere, unless you want your sins to be known throughout the village. Do you want to say anything else, Sorina?'

'Will the house fall down if I tell what happened to me? Will the bloodless one come and kill me?'

'The house won't fall down but maybe the bloodless one will come for the priest,' said Edith.

She watched as the man mopped his forehead with his handkerchief.

Sorina stood. 'I went to help at the inn when the hunting party came up from town last summer.'

'What has that to do with anything?' said the priest. 'We're here because the butcher has been murdered.'

'You'll be quiet,' said the mayor, 'and you'll listen.'

Sorina bit her lip. Her legs were shaking.

'You can sit,' said Edith.

'No,' said Sorina and started again. 'When the hunting party came last year, the innkeeper needed extra help. I cleaned the rooms and changed the bed linen. Later, as I was leaving, my grandfather came up the stairs with a young man. I remember he wore round glasses – he took them off when he… when he…' She took a breath. 'He was drunk and he muttered something to Grandpa. Grandpa said to me, "Why don't you be sweet to this man," and he went away. Do I have to say more?'

'No,' said Edith. 'Unless you want to.'

Sorina thought for a moment. 'When I went to leave, my grandfather told me not to make a scene, that no one would believe me. He said that if I said a word, one word, the bloodless would come for me. I confessed to the priest. I told him I was having a baby. I told no one else. I trusted him. Then my grandfather said he knew and he wouldn't tell my mother – it would be our secret, and he would help me.

'I was so happy to be rid of the baby. When I started to

clean Grandpa's house he insisted… he insisted I wore his mother's shawl. He said again it was our secret and if I ever told then his mother would come for me and take me to the graveyard. When I was pregnant again, he beat me then took me to the doctor. I never, ever want another man to touch me.' She looked at the priest. 'You are… disgusting!' She shouted the last word.

'The truth shines,' said Edith. 'You can't keep it in the shadows for the sun will always find its moment to bring it to the light. Priest, you are trusted by so many and you abused that trust.'

The mayor said to the priest, 'You are a coward and the crime you have committed is beyond any words I have. You will leave this village as soon as you've buried the butcher. There are, so I believe, signs that the dead come back as the bloodless. You, Priest, had better take care. They feed on cowards. And you, Doctor, you will go when a replacement has been found for you.'

'Now tell me, Mayor,' said Edith. 'How did the butcher die?'

'Suicide,' said the mayor.

'Doctor?'

'Ah – suicide,' said the doctor.

'Una?'

'I shot him.'

'Sorina?'

'My mother had the courage to kill a monster.'

'Misha?'

'The bastard killed himself.'

'Priest?'

He didn't answer immediately. Then, 'Suicide.'

'The truth,' said Edith, 'is that the butcher is dead.'

# CHAPTER THIRTY

## CHURCH BELLS RANG

'Who's going to tell the bees and the animals in the stable that the butcher's dead?' said Sorina. 'Someone must otherwise another misfortune is bound to happen.'

The men looked uncomfortable.

'I should fetch my mother,' said Misha.

He left the house by the yard gate. A crowd had gathered outside.

'We heard a gunshot,' said a woman. 'What's happened?'

His head down, Misha pushed through and the villagers, getting no response, turned their attention back to the house.

Misha felt it first in the pit of his stomach and it rose inside him until his face broke out in a smile. Finally, he was free of that man. The day was brighter than the day before. Last night Lena had told him how much she loved him. He put his hand to his beard – his hair had grown long. He would go to the barber's; this was a new beginning.

First he went to the cabinet maker's house and was glad

to find that the old drunk wasn't yet up. Quickly Misha ran up to the attic room and retrieved his revolver. He'd bought it in case he needed to defend himself against his grandfather and had taken it with him up the mountain and fired it once for practice. He checked the chambers – one missing bullet – and tucked the weapon in his belt, under his coat.

At his mother's house he was greeted by the smell of fresh bread and coffee. Vanda was alarmed to see him.

'Is it Edith? Has something happened to her?'

'No, Mother. Not Edith. It's the butcher.'

'What about him?'

'He's dead.'

For a moment Misha thought she was going to faint. He caught her and helped her to a chair.

'Dead?' she said.

'Yes.' Misha knelt beside her. 'Una shot him. But the mayor believes it's suicide.'

'It's justice, that's what it is,' said Vanda. 'Long overdue justice.' She stood and wrapped her shawl round her. 'I've dreamed of this day for a long time and never thought it would happen.' She put her arm through her son's. 'Una won't be arrested, will she?'

'I don't think so. Though she keeps saying she shot him.'

'Then she'll be arrested and charged and...'

'Mother, I've never seen the mayor look more relieved, and the doctor and even the priest have agreed to say the butcher killed himself.'

'The priest? That shit,' said Vanda.

It was as if all the village were waiting at the butcher's house. Vanda drove them aside as she would geese. Inside, the cuckoo clock struck the hour.

'I want to see him,' said Vanda.

She followed Misha into the bedroom and stood silent for a moment then said, quietly, 'Hell is too good a place for him.'

The sound of Sorina's hysterical laughter made her look up and she hurried to the kitchen. Misha closed the bedroom door behind her. The butcher had ruined the lives of too many people and Misha was determined that his dead finger should point at no one but himself. Carefully, Misha placed his revolver where he imagined it would have fallen if the butcher had fired it.

In the kitchen, Vanda gathered Sorina to her and sat her down as the girl's laughter turned to tears.

'I shot him,' said Una to her sister.

'Not a day too soon,' said Vanda.

'I refused to hear you... I remembered the shawl... I remembered you wearing it and my...' Her words were lost in sobs.

Vanda pulled her chair closer to Una's. 'It's a pity there wasn't a spare bullet for him,' she said, nodding at the priest.

'The priest will be leaving the village,' said the mayor.

'Good,' said Vanda. 'Could he move out of my sight? Why doesn't he wait in the bedroom with my father? Perhaps there are some words he'd like to mumble over him.'

'Women,' muttered the priest.

Edith caught his arm. 'What did you say?' she said.

'I said, "Women."'

'You owe us women an apology – you owe the whole village an apology for your behaviour. You should stand up in church and say sorry for the pain and misery you and the butcher caused Sorina, caused all of us. You terrified Lena's mother into keeping her daughter a prisoner. You accused Flora of being a whore. And you tried to force me into marrying an evil man. The list of your sins is endless.'

The priest yanked his arm away. 'I said I would agree that the butcher's death was suicide. And I will as long as I'm allowed to leave the village peacefully.'

Misha came quietly into the kitchen and stood behind his mother, putting his hand on her shoulder.

'Excuse me, Priest,' said Sorina, 'if a man commits suicide, he's more likely to come back as one of the bloodless, isn't he? And even if you read a service at the side of the butcher's grave and sprinkle it with holy water, it won't stop him coming back to find you and take you with him, will it?'

'But we all know the butcher didn't take his own life,' said the priest.

'But surely he did?' It was the hard voice of the miller. No one had seen or heard the elder come in.

'There is no doubt in my mind that it was suicide,' the mayor said boldly.

'Of course it was, he used this,' said the miller, holding up the revolver. 'It was on the floor by the bed.'

The mayor was speechless, baffled as to why neither the doctor, the priest nor himself had noticed it.

'Perhaps, Mayor,' said the miller. 'You should talk to the villagers.'

'Yes, yes, I will give an address in the square in half an hour,' he said, trying to cover his surprise.

'That's as it should be,' said the miller. 'I'll let it be known.'

He went outside and could be heard giving instructions to the crowd.

'Where did the revolver come from?' said the doctor to the mayor.

'We missed it, didn't we, Doctor?' said the mayor. 'It must have been among the bedclothes and fallen to the floor.'

'Yes,' said the doctor, 'that must be it.'

'It was found,' said Misha, 'that's the important thing.'

*

The blacksmith's cart arrived at the butcher's house fifteen minutes later and Edith let it into the yard. The blacksmith and Misha lifted the body of the butcher onto a sheet and covered it with another.

'May I come with you?' the priest asked the blacksmith. He had no desire to face his congregation. The sooner he was gone from here the better.

'Yes,' said the blacksmith. 'I'm only going to the forge.'

'I know,' said the priest.

Misha opened the gates and the cart trundled off. The

priest, sitting beside the body of the butcher, appeared to have shrunk in size. Children ran behind, pulling faces at him.

Half an hour later, the death of the butcher was no longer a rumour. Women, men and children came out into the sunshine and stood in the square in the morning light, waiting for something to be said to mark the momentous event. Usually the butcher would take the lead but that strange morning it was the mayor.

'Ladies and gentlemen,' he said, 'I have to inform you that the butcher has taken his own life.'

There was a gasp of surprise, then a stunned silence.

'Is he really dead?' asked someone.

'Yes,' said the mayor.

'Does that mean we'll have to pay what we owe him?' said another voice.

'Yes, what about the money?' asked one of the farmers.

The mayor had discussed the matter with Vanda and Misha before he'd ventured out to give his address. They'd both said the debts should go with the butcher's dying.

'Anyone owing money to the butcher will not have to pay back a penny,' said the mayor. 'That is the wish of his two daughters and his grandson.'

'Are you sure about that?' asked another.

'Yes, now go home,' said the mayor.

'But what about the priest?' said the farmer.

The question surprised the mayor. 'What about the priest?' he said.

'He's as bad as the butcher, they worked together. He'll come for the money.'

'Yes,' agreed another. 'He'll come and he'll threaten us.'

'That won't happen,' said the mayor. 'Once the butcher has been buried, the priest will leave, and a new priest found.'

There was a shout of heartfelt joy.

The mayor realised how isolated he'd been from this community. He should have stepped in long ago. He felt ashamed to think that he hadn't had the courage to stop the butcher. He caught sight of his wife in the crowd and thought, I should have had the courage to tell her about the letters. She would have stood up to the butcher. She's stronger than I am. He looked up as the church bells rang out into the mountain. Freedom, they pealed.

# CHAPTER THIRTY-ONE

## THE LETTER

Not long after Edith arrived home, she found the cabinet maker's bed hadn't been slept in. All that day a party was out searching for him. When Edith returned in the afternoon she was struck by the stillness of the house, a stillness it had never possessed before, and she knew that the old fool was dead.

Perhaps that was what had woken her so early. It had nothing do with the butcher. She sat on the verandah steps. The hens already seemed plumper and one had laid an egg as if in gratitude for being rescued.

Edith hadn't eaten all day and was thinking about supper when Georgeta came into the yard with a basket of food and wine.

'I heard your father is missing. I've brought you this,' she said. 'It's long overdue. I would've come sooner if I hadn't been looking after my son.'

Edith took the basket into the kitchen, found two glasses

and opened the bottle. The day had been a rehearsal for the summer to come and they sat on the verandah as the sun lingered, golden in its warmth.

'I wonder what your grandmother would have made of all this,' said Georgeta.

'Not much,' said Edith.

'She would have been very proud of you. It took courage to do what you did.'

'Not as much as it took Una to do what she did.'

'Una will get better in time,' said Georgeta. 'But I don't know about Sorina.'

'How is your son?' Edith asked.

'He recovered almost the minute he heard the butcher was dead. He confessed he'd lied, that he'd never seen you as one of the bloodless. He told me the butcher had made him say those things. He refuses to tell me more and, if I'm honest, I don't want to know. But my husband says we must talk and that is rare. Usually it's he who talks and I who listen.'

Edith put her feet up on the carved balustrade of the verandah and said,

'I wasn't related to the woman I called Grandmother.'

'I know,' said Georgeta. 'She told me.'

'Did she tell you anything else?'

'That she had a fearful row with the cabinet maker, that she said over her dead body would you marry the butcher.'

'Go on,' said Edith.

'Before she came here, she lived down the mountain and made her living going from village to village telling stories.

In the summer she would travel with the circus. She was very fond of your mother.'

'Did you meet my mother?'

'Yes, once. She was pretty – not dark like you but fair, pale as snow. Your grandmother took your mother in when she left the cabinet maker. She returned to him not out of love but out of guilt. He pleaded with her, promised to be a better man. The spring before you were born, there was talk that he had another woman in a village not far from here and that summer your grandmother took your mother travelling with her. She craved a baby as a starving man wants for food and, when she came back, she was pregnant.'

'Perhaps I did come from the goblin market,' said Edith.

'It doesn't matter that your grandmother wasn't related to you. It was she who brought you up. You are a remarkable woman in no small part due to her. Blood or no blood.'

\*

Three days later the cabinet maker hadn't been found and the village elders and the mayor agreed that the search for him should be called off.

As one of the elders said, 'The mountain gives back its dead when it's ready and no amount of looking will change that.'

Edith was surprised at how little she felt; just an acceptance that the cabinet maker was gone. All she could hope for was that death had met him kindly and she suspected it had.

In the space between the butcher's death and his burial,

villagers began to talk about him and what he had done to them. They came to Edith's house to watch Misha make the coffin; the sight of it enough to reassure them the butcher wasn't coming back.

'The earth won't weep for his grave,' said a farmer.

Two days before the butcher was to be buried the blacksmith came to collect the coffin and bring Flora to see Edith. She was carrying a parcel.

'Better than he deserves,' said the blacksmith as they loaded the coffin onto the cart.

Misha went with him to the forge, leaving Flora and Edith sitting outside. Edith lifted her face to the sun.

'This time next week we will be married, and I will see our daughter again,' said Flora. 'Oh Edith – this is a new beginning.'

Edith thought back to last spring, just before she met Demetrius, when she felt it to be full of new beginnings. She enjoyed hearing Flora speak; a tumble of words colliding with one another, accompanied by a bush full of sparrows arguing, each with a chorus for Flora's happiness.

'This is for you,' said Flora. 'I charged the butcher far too much for the wedding gown.' Edith opened the parcel to find a dress and a long travelling coat. 'I thought you should come and stay with us. I've written down the address. And don't forget to bring your embroidery.'

'Flora, they are too beautiful. Thank you. But...'

'No buts. Just remember to bring some of your embroidery with you.'

'Why?'

'Because it's all the fashion and rich ladies pay ridiculous money for exceptional needlework.'

*

It was late afternoon and Edith had a stew slowly cooking when Misha returned from the forge. He had been to the barber's on the way back and his winter beard and his long hair were gone. A clean-shaven, handsome young man stood before her.

'I'm going to ask Lena's mother if we can be married as soon as we have a new priest.'

'Has Lena agreed?'

'She has,' said Misha, smiling.

'Then ask Lena and her mother to come to supper with us to celebrate.'

She heard him close the yard gate then went to her father's room. She'd changed the sheets on the bed and had collected the empty bottles hidden under it when Misha came into the kitchen.

'It's no good,' he said, furiously. 'She called me an... an idiot... said she'd never let her daughter marry the village simpleton.' He pushed his fists into his eyes and Edith could see the broken child in him again. 'That's what I am – that's what I'll always be. The dirt from the butcher's boots.'

Edith pulled his hands away.

'Misha,' she said, 'listen to me. Remember what Demetrius

told you – you mustn't let yourself be defined by the butcher's word.'

'I might as well have made the coffin for myself.'

'Misha, would you put the dumplings in the stew and lay the table?'

'Of course. I'm sorry.'

She put her arm round him. 'It was no fool who thought to put the revolver in the butcher's bedroom. Does Lena think you're a fool?'

'No.'

'So, add the dumplings in five minutes.'

Lena's mother opened the door a crack at Edith's knock. Knowing she would close it again, Edith called, 'Lena,' and Lena, who had been in tears at what her mother had said to Misha, rushed down the stairs, pushed her mother out the way and put her arms round her friend.

'I've come to invite you and your mother to supper,' said Edith.

'Lena's going nowhere,' said the widow. 'She's not having supper at your house while that lovesick idiot is there.'

Edith gazed at the widow and took her time. 'You'll regret this,' she said slowly. 'Your granddaughter will be born, and Lena and her husband won't want you in their house. They won't want their beautiful and clever daughter to ever hear that word. You'll be alone here while your daughter and your son-in-law live a happy and prosperous life. And you'll have a corrupt butcher to thank for your loneliness.'

'How dare you speak to me like that? You are a disgrace!

The way you came back into the village – I saw you – a heathen.'

'Please, Mother,' said Lena. She took Edith's arm.

'If you go... I wash my hands of you!'

But the widow found herself shouting at a closed wooden door.

\*

'That was better than stealing cherries when we were young,' said Lena, laughing.

'Much, much better,' said Edith.

Misha was waiting on the verandah and Edith left them together and went to feed the hens. She thought, I should have said fifteen minutes before he put the dumplings in. Never mind. She gave up worrying about supper and walked down to the stream and sat a while, staring through the orchard at the snow-topped mountain. She had a feeling that Demetrius was near her again.

\*

Vanda and Una had decided that afternoon to clear out the butcher's house, something they wanted to do together. Sorina had asked to help and the three of them had built a fire in the yard from all the furniture that had been associated in their minds with the butcher's mother. Her shawl lay on top of the pile. They set fire to it and watched the flames devour it, hungry for the feast.

Before they left, Sorina said, 'There's something Edith should have.' Una went with her into the bedroom and from under the bed Sorina pulled a pair of boots. Curled inside one was a letter. 'They belonged to the shepherd.'

*

That night, the moon rose, massive in its roundness, and sat for a moment on top of the church spire.

No one knew how the blaze started but it was thought that a spark from the fire that Una, Vanda and Sorina had made in the butcher's yard might have been the cause. It was indeed windy that afternoon. But whatever it was, the butcher's house was well and truly alight. It stood apart from the other houses so there was no great urgency to put out the flames. Edith saw the sparks rise into the sky and, as Misha and Lena had no interest in anything except each other, she joined the rest of the villagers watching the butcher's house burn. It was an hypnotic sight and had to it a justice that she hadn't known was needed before she saw the house in flames.

Vanda found her in the crowd.

'These were under the butcher's bed,' she said, giving her a pair of boots. 'There's a letter tucked in one of them.'

Edith remembered the day she had first seen Demetrius, the boots next to him on the bench outside the cobbler's. She held them tight to her, too stunned to think what to say.

The priest watched the fire from a window of his house. It was proof, he was certain, that the butcher would come back as a bloodless one. He had seen him in his nightmares, the wax from a candle dripping onto dead flesh.

\*

It was nearing midnight when Edith returned home. The house quiet, she put the boots on a chair and took out the letter. It was written in a clear hand. She poured herself a glass of plum brandy and read it.

\*

*My beloved Edith,*

*I am not writing this letter to make you sad. I hope we will be laughing together, and you will tell me what foolishness it was to put these words on paper. But if I know you, as I believe I do, you will understand what I am about to say. I have had a premonition. It happened on the day I met the butcher. I thought it was to do with your fate but now I am sure it was a foreshadowing of my own death. My mistake was to imagine the butcher as a pantomime villain. Too late, I realised why you were worried. You are far too intuitive to dismiss him lightly. Never did I imagine he could stop us from being together.*

*My love, if I return then tell me I am a fool, but if I don't, know this: I have never loved anyone as I have you. Because it is night it doesn't mean I am not here. When the dawn comes, you will see me again. Don't put me on a pedestal. Don't make me into a little god of a future we didn't have. Live your life, relish whatever it might bring you. May it bring you the wisdom to love again, enjoy your beautiful body and may you have many lovers to kiss you and love you in all the ways I cannot.*

*My love for you will not be frozen by death; the waiting will not be marked by years. No clock can give me time. I will be here, and that is where you will find me. Be free. I put no chains on you. To truly love is to let go, and by doing so, I know you will return when the winter comes, and the days draw in on a life lived with passion. Do not feel guilty for the footsteps you take without me.*

*With my blessing, with all my love, choose life, Edith. Not for both of us – my days are nearly spent – but for yourself. Fill your lungs with mountain air, tell your stories, let them take you on a journey.*

*My love, my heart, you are in my soul.*

# CHAPTER THIRTY-TWO

## THE CROSSROADS

Edith couldn't sleep. She read the letter again and again and knew that the sorrow of losing Demetrius was the sharpest of thorns. His gift to her, his love, was the rose. If it had been she who'd died, she would have wanted the same for him: not to waste his days in dreams of what could never be. She would have wanted him to play his violin, to love again. This letter told her that Demetrius understood her completely. He had seen the wild woman, the traveller within her, long before she had seen it in herself.

I'm not expecting to find my happiness in marriage and children, she thought. I know that's not my story. Demetrius gave me a mirror so that I might see the infinite possibilities of love. Perhaps to truly love is to accept there will be change and only through change can love grow.

In the honeyed dawn of a new day she felt there was hope. His words were freedom. Hadn't she stared death in the face?

Now she said aloud, 'Give me the wisdom to be brave. Don't let me make the past my cage.'

She stood, stretched out her arms and knew she was ready to leave the village.

The coffee was on the stove, the bread in the oven and she went out to feed the hens. She found two eggs as the cock crowed in the new day. As she went back to the house the sky was turning gun-black and fat droplets of rain were falling. When she reached the verandah, the rain was cascading onto the tiles.

'A good morning for the burial,' said Misha coming out of the bedroom. 'Lena's still asleep.'

Edith shook off the rain and poured the coffee. 'Do you want an egg?' she said.

They ate breakfast together.

The rain was pouring down and thunder growled its way into the yard.

'You'll get wet,' said Edith.

She found her father's old umbrella which he'd never used and now would never need. She gave it to Misha and followed him to the gate, her shawl over her head, and watched him carrying an invisible wreath of rage to lay on the butcher's coffin.

At the crossroads the blacksmith, huddled under an oilskin, waited in his cart for Misha. In the back, next to the coffin, sat the priest and next to the priest was the priest's trunk. While they waited the priest tried to negotiate a price with the blacksmith to take him to the main road that led to the town.

The blacksmith refused. 'You spread lies about Flora,' he said simply. 'Why should I do anything for you?'

'Out of kindness?' suggested the priest.

'As kindness and cruelty were both the same to you and the butcher, who's to say I'm not being kind?'

The priest didn't say another word.

The horse stamped, steam coming out of its nostrils. It moved forward slightly when it saw Misha walking towards them.

'Good morning,' said the blacksmith and gave Misha a hand up onto the cart.

They set off to an open field, well away from church, where the butcher's grave had been dug. Lightning flashed yellow across the grey sky and thunder rolled down from the mountain. A pungent smell of garlic came from the coffin as Misha and the blacksmith lifted it from the cart and slid it into the flooded grave.

As the priest stood shivering by the grave, the rain stopped and the sun broke through the windmill clouds, sending out sharp rays of sunshine.

'Aren't you going to pay your respects?' asked the priest.

Neither Misha nor the blacksmith said a word. They walked away and waited under a chestnut tree while the priest gave the service alone.

'He put a stake through the butcher's heart,' said the blacksmith, rolling his tobacco. 'And there's more garlic in that coffin than you'd stuff a goose with.'

At last the priest stood back and Misha and the blacksmith

covered the coffin with earth. They were pressing down the tufts of grass when they heard the distant sound of drums, trumpets and cymbals.

'What's that?' said the priest, a look of fear on his face.

The blacksmith, the tallest of the three, could see the top of a tattered banner winding its way up the path to the village.

'Sounds like the devil's music,' said the priest.

'You of all people should know,' said the blacksmith.

The banner came into view. It read 'Zamfir's Circus'. One more turn in the dirt road and there came a motley collection of people in faded clothes that once had been bright. Some were on horseback, some on foot and one led a bear. They were followed by three lumbering houses on wheels. The procession came to a halt and out of one of the houses stepped a man. He was striking in looks; his hair was dark and tousled, he wore a black frock coat with red and green checked trousers, an embroidered waistcoat and pointed red boots. He was carrying a top hat.

He walked with energy towards them and seeing the priest said, 'Is this a funeral?'

'Yes,' said the priest.

'Where are the mourners? Where's the feast?' He looked from Misha to the blacksmith then the newly covered grave and said, 'Ah. I see. He took his own life.'

'It's none of your business,' said the priest.

'My name is Zamfir and this is my circus. I know you, Priest. Yes, indeed. It was you and the butcher who turned my father away last year.'

'We told him we didn't want any gypsies in our village,' said the priest.

'We are called Tzigane,' said Zamfir. 'The word gypsy is an insult.'

'Can we help you?' asked Misha.

'Is there a doctor in the village? A trapeze artist fell and broke her wrist.'

Half an hour later the circus was off the road, the caravans parked and Zamfir had helped the young girl into the back of the blacksmith's cart. He climbed in with her and, as the cart set off for the village, he watched the priest pulling his trunk behind him down the mountain road.

'Was it the butcher you buried?' he asked.

# CHAPTER THIRTY-THREE

## THE FIRST STEP

Edith knew if she didn't leave tomorrow, she never would. There must, she thought, be an unspoken order to the ritual of breaking free; actions that had to be performed in the right sequence before the cage door opened wide enough to release her. Instinctively she understood that just to walk away would mean that she would be trailing the past behind her and in that there would be no freedom. She'd told Misha she would stay until his wedding, but by then all her courage would have vanished, her feet glued to the ground.

She counted the thunder that morning as a sign. In a village riddled with superstition, thunder on the day of a burial meant the devil attended the butcher's funeral. The counterbalance to the end of a life must be the celebration of something new.

'I'm going to give you a betrothal supper,' said Edith to Lena. 'Tonight. And it won't involve fish,' she added. The idea wasn't met with enthusiasm. 'You do want to be married to Misha?'

'Yes of course. Yes,' said Lena who was already worried about what the village gossips were saying about her living in the cabinet maker's house. 'Yes,' she said again. 'But I think it should be done properly. Your father is still missing and…'

'Don't be a goose. He's dead and it's not a valid excuse. Look at you. You want to marry Misha, you're having his baby, he loves you, and I hope you feel the same.'

'I do.'

'It's Thursday – a lucky day.'

'Yes, it is,' agreed Lena. 'Though all the days of the week are full of perils. Anyway, no one would come. And we haven't a lot of food. It's kind of you but it isn't practical.'

'It is,' said Edith firmly. 'And it will happen tonight. If no one else comes then I'll drink your health alone. But they will come.'

'How many?'

'Eleven or twelve – I don't know. I'm not inviting the elders.'

'Oh dear. But… perhaps, if you told one of your grandmother's stories…'

'Why would that make a difference?'

'People will always come to hear a story and the elders wouldn't be so offended.'

Edith shook her head. This is why I can't stay, she thought. This endless petty superstition that makes everybody scared to look on the world outside.

'Why does it matter what anyone thinks? You're happy yet

you subject your happiness to old wives' tales. Wednesdays and Fridays are days when no one must use needles or scissors, or bake bread. Tuesdays are unlucky for spinning, and at sunset evil spirits abound. Thursdays and Saturdays are lucky days so you may wash and spin. But be careful, the devil is always waiting at the bottom of the garden. Tell me, what will happen if we have your betrothal supper tonight? Will the house fall down?'

'Of course not,' said Lena. 'But the hens might not lay for a year.'

Edith laughed. 'Have you thought that it was these ancient beliefs that gave the power to the butcher to keep you prisoner? And by believing in them, we give power to the elders and make monsters of men?'

'Are you cross with me?'

'No, Lena, I'm cross that you can't see what you have and how lucky you are. Instead you act as if you've done something wrong.'

There was a knock on the door and Edith went to open it.

'I've been thinking,' said Georgeta, coming inside. 'It's none of my business but I feel that there should be…'

'…A party to celebrate Lena and Misha's engagement,' said Edith. She led Georgeta into the parlour. 'Yes, that's my suggestion. And maybe,' she muttered, 'Lena's mother would come round to the idea of the marriage.'

'You don't think it's a little hasty?' said Lena.

'Not at all,' said Georgeta. 'I think a celebration is much needed. I'll bring food and my maids to help.'

'Both of them – and the cook?' said Edith. 'Will the mayor manage without someone at his beck and call?'

'I doubt it,' said Georgeta and laughed.

Lena was so surprised by this sudden turn of events that she couldn't think what to say except a quiet 'Thank you.'

\*

Misha returned to find women cooking and the kitchen filled with laughter.

'We are having a betrothal supper,' said Lena.

'This is for us?' said Misha.

It occurred to Edith that this was the first time in his life that Misha had ever been at the centre of a celebration.

'Is it true that a circus is camped just outside the village?' Georgeta asked him.

'A circus?' said Edith.

'That's right,' said Misha. 'It turned up after the burial. The priest heard it coming and thought it was the devil. The blacksmith and I brought the proprietor and his trapeze artist into the village. She's injured her wrist.'

\*

Taking a basket, Edith walked down to the stream by the orchard. The air was heady with lilac blossom and she had filled her basket with enough blooms to decorate the table when a figure in a tall top hat appeared on the other side of the stream. In the golden light of the early evening she remembered how once Demetrius had stood waiting for her there.

She jumped when the man called to her.

'I'm looking for the storyteller.'

'I'm the storyteller's granddaughter,' she said. 'I'm Edith.'

'My name is Zamfir. I own the circus,' he said. 'Is the storyteller here? One of my artists has broken her wrist and without someone else to entertain the crowd, we'll be off the road for longer than I can afford.' He looked at the lilac blossom. 'What are you celebrating?'

'A betrothal,' said Edith.

'Are you to be married?'

She laughed. 'No. I'm to tell a story. My grandmother was the storyteller – she told me about your circus. She died over five years ago.'

Zamfir said nothing but nodded.

'You're welcome to come tonight,' said Edith. 'I will be telling one of her stories.' The circus owner tipped his hat. 'The house is up there,' she added, turning from him to point to it.

When she looked back he was gone.

*

Lena was brushing her hair before the guests arrived when Edith brought her the clothes that she'd embroidered for her own wedding.

'These are for you,' said Edith. 'A wedding present.'

'You can't give them to me,' said Lena. 'They're for your wedding.'

Edith said nothing but helped Lena to dress.

'You're leaving, I know you are,' said Lena. 'That's why you've given me these. Don't go, please.'

'I can't stay,' said Edith. 'I couldn't stay here without being married and I couldn't marry a man I didn't love. You should understand that. I haven't told Misha, but I've left a letter for you both. If you want to, you can live here. Misha would have the workshop and could make a decent living.'

Lena put her arms round Edith. 'Thank you,' she said.

'Not a word to Misha. Can you do that?'

'You kept my secret. What you ask is such a small thing.' She sniffed. 'You will write, won't you?'

'Don't cry,' said Edith. 'Goodness knows what misfortune befalls a bride who cries at her betrothal supper.'

*

Twenty people came to the supper. The mayor came and raised a glass to new beginnings. Even Lena's mother came. And near the end of the meal, three musicians appeared on the verandah.

'Zamfir sent us to play for you,' said the tall man with the cello. 'He said you're going to tell a story.'

Lena's mother said, 'That's the only reason I came – to hear a story.'

For a moment there was an awkward silence but then, seeing the widow was smiling, everyone laughed.

'A story,' said Georgeta. 'Yes, Edith – tell us a story.'

More chairs were found for the musicians and more wine was poured.

That evening Edith cast a spell over the party, telling the story of a shepherd and his bride. The musicians played to fit the tale – the bang of the drum for the villain, the violin and the cello for the souls of the hero and heroine – and Edith seamlessly brought out the light and the dark, as all good weavers of words should. She fashioned the story out of her grandmother's many tales and stitched it together with her own wit into something that chimed with all who were present. She was pleased to see she brought both laughter and a tear to the eye and as she came to the end she picked up the violin and played a last note that fell into the silence.

The guests clapped and called for more.

'One is enough,' said Edith.

The evening drew to an end. The air had turned cold and the guests and the musicians congratulated the lovers and left into the dark of a spring night.

Flora said, 'We're leaving tomorrow. Be at the forge at dawn if you want to come with us. And don't forget your embroidery.'

Edith closed the gate and found she was disappointed that Zamfir hadn't come.

# CHAPTER THIRTY-FOUR

## A MYRIAD OF STARS

The house fell silent. Edith put on her fur hat with the antlers and her grandmother's coat of fables and poured a glass of wine. In her mind she heard the music of the violin. She went outside. The sky was a canopy of stars and she put out her arms and began to spin, round and round, until she saw Zamfir watching her.

'I have a story for you,' he said. 'One I don't think you've heard before.'

Edith went to take off her hat, but he said, 'Keep it on – it suits you.'

She offered him a glass of wine.

'People have the queerest idea about us circus folk,' Zamfir said as they sat down on the verandah steps. He took a sip of his wine. 'They think we're immoral and that we drink ourselves to death after a life of vice. It's not true. We live simple lives and we look after each other. I think you know how it is when you're seen in a light that doesn't reflect the truth of who you are. You have a gift with story; tonight you used three that I know well and changed them and made them into your own brew.'

'You heard me?'

'Yes. But I have a story for you. It's about your beginning, where you came from.'

Edith thought of when Demetrius had told her how the violin had come into the world.

'Our circus always had a storyteller,' said Zamfir, 'and the finest of them was the woman you knew as your grand-mother. In the summer she would travel with us, telling stories that were acted by the clowns. One summer the storyteller brought a young woman with her. She was slight with snow-white skin. Her husband, the cabinet maker, had found another woman in a village further down the mountain and the storyteller hoped that after a few months away the young woman might find the strength to leave him for good.

'One evening after a show when we were gathered for music and a meal, a stranger came and stood to look into the fire. It's said he was a handsome devil – dark eyes, black hair – and the young woman couldn't stop looking at him. He went to where she was sitting and said, "You will never have a child with your husband." She had stood up, furious to be spoken to in that way, and went to slap him. The stranger was fast, he caught her arm and kissed her. Never had anyone seen such a startled expression on any woman's face. The storyteller told him, "Enough of this nonsense."

'He didn't move. The music stopped, all went quiet and he said, "Old woman, you will bring up the child. She will be like me, she'll have the power to walk between two worlds."

'The storyteller raised her hands to the heavens when she saw the young woman walk away with him. But she was confident that in the morning sense and reason would return.

'It didn't. When it was time for the circus to move on the young woman said she was staying. After the summer the storyteller went back for her and saw straight away she was with child. And they went home.

'Six months later a midwife called the storyteller to the house of the cabinet maker. His wife, the young woman, had died and the child was sickly and not likely to live. The cabinet maker wanted the storyteller to take the baby, saying girls had no value, they took land away from you and brought little in return. But the storyteller stayed and became your grandmother, and she poured her stories into you. Now,' said Zamfir, 'I've told you your beginning, tell me your end.'

Edith looked up at the myriad of stars and thought about the power of a story to define a past or predict a future, of the infinite possibilities of what lay ahead. One thing was certain: come the new day she would be leaving. The rest was unknown, except for the end of her story.

'Do you really want to hear it?' she said.

'Yes,' he said.

She was quiet for a while and when she did speak it felt to him as if the night itself was talking, all too aware of the dawn to come.

'This is yet to happen which has never happened and will happen again.

'An old woman returns to the village she was born in after years of travelling. There is one journey left and this she has saved for the last. She has roamed far, telling her stories, some years have been better than others. She has left the man she lived with. He loved her more than she could ever love him; some say that was what kept him close to her. They parted at a railway station. He knew this day would come because she had told him this much of their future.

'She finds a house outside the village, she keeps a sheep for company and promises it will never smell mutton cooking. Villagers come to her, feeling her stories calm a trouble mind, put right a wrong, and there she stays until the sheep dies and autumn turns to winter. She knows the snow is coming. She has waited for this snow for a long time. One morning she wakes to the chiming of the snow, the music of a winter sky. She leaves a note on the table as she did many years ago when she first left her house to go travelling. This time she won't take the violin, there's no point. In her mind she has made this journey a thousand times. She has no fear of the frost, no fear of the snow. All that matters is that she finds the two dancing fir trees.

'The day is drawing in and never once does she doubt the trees. She hears the wolf howl, hears the bear growl and is not afraid. When the moon rises the two mighty fir trees stand before her like gossiping ladies in their dancing white skirts. She pushes through their soft caresses until she is in the clearing with the wooden cabin.

'The moonlight shines silver on him; he is beautiful, untouched by time, and all age falls from her as she goes to him. He puts his hand to her face. His eyes are the blue of a winter's sky and she knows she is home.'

# ACKNOWLEDGEMENTS

I would like to acknowledge the lobster. First, I must thank Clio Cornish, who over lunch, suggested I write a story set in snow – though at the time my mind went completely blank while the lobster congealed on its bed of noodles.

It took a while to come up with the story until Emily Gerard's excellent book *The Land Beyond the Forest* led me to the location. My thanks to her and to other writers whose adventures and pens took them among the Saxon and Roma peoples of the region.

I would like to thank my dear friend Julia Paton for her generous spirit, Jacky Bateman for her work on the manuscript without which I would be lost in the forest, and my new editor, Finn Cotton. It has been a pleasure to work with him. Grateful thanks to my agent Catherine Clarke, and to Lisa Milton for publishing this book.

Special thanks go to my daughter, Freya, whose wisdom and philosophy are second to none. She always sets me on the right path when the snow becomes too deep.

Sally Gardner
Hastings, June 2020

## ONE PLACE. MANY STORIES

Bold, innovative and
empowering publishing.

FOLLOW US ON:

@HQStories